MW01253111

No Wake Zone

No Wake Zone

A Novel

JP Rodriguez

CANADA

Copyright © 2024 by JP Rodriguez

All rights reserved. No part of this book may be used or reproduced
in any manner whatsoever without the prior written permission of the publisher,
except in the case of brief quotations embodied in reviews.

*Publisher's note: This book is a work of fiction. Names, characters, places and
incidents are either the product of the author's imagination or are used
fictitiously, and any resemblance to actual persons living or dead
is entirely coincidental.*

Library and Archives Canada Cataloguing in Publication

Title: No wake zone : a novel / JP Rodriguez.

Names: Rodriguez, J. P., 1973- author.

Identifiers: Canadiana (print) 20240382595 | Canadiana (ebook) 20240382609 |
ISBN 9781989689745 (softcover) | ISBN 9781989689783 (EPUB)

Subjects: LCGFT: Novels.

Classification: LCC PS8635.O3745 N62 2024 | DDC C813/.6—dc23

Printed and bound in Canada on 100% recycled paper.

Now Or Never Publishing
901, 163 Street
Surrey, British Columbia
Canada V4A 9T8

nonpublishing.com
Fighting Words.

We gratefully acknowledge the support of the Canada Council for the Arts
and the British Columbia Arts Council for our publishing program.

To my sweet, sweet Parker and Maple

"Civilization is a race between education and disaster."

~ H.G. Wells

"No man chooses evil because it is evil; he only mistakes it for happiness, the good he seeks."

~ Mary Wollstonecraft

"WANT TO KNOW the craziest conception of the future? From people on the real cutting edge of this stuff?"

"You think my *geezer* brain can handle it?"

"I think you've proven yourself."

"Then go."

"Our minds will meld with a massive supercomputer, with endless storage and reproducibility. And we'll all be the same VR space. And it'll be all about experiences. We'll trade in experiences because they'll be completely sharable. And the boring ones, the boring memories, will never be used, so the OS just cuts them out over time because they haven't been accessed in years and are just a waste of space. And those best experiences will be shared and shared and become our own memories, and over time, we'll all generally share the same memories and we'll all essentially be one. Isn't that wild?"

"It makes my brain hurt."

"When I was a kid I used to lie awake trying to think of what it was that made me me, and not someone else. And were we all maybe ultimately the same, because thinking of everyone actually being different and separate made *my* brain hurt. I wondered if we weren't just all crumbs split off a grand consciousness, some Humpty Dumpty God. And now I wonder, as we increasingly connect and share and overlap, maybe we're putting that grand single consciousness back together again, all joining up and reassembling, losing ourselves but becoming all."

"…Must you?"

0.

I NEVER SAID, and am not saying here, that I'm the greatest writer in the world. But you're going to be clamouring to know this sort of stuff, this story, and I guess I kind of want you to know it, so here goes. And there is that short story I wrote for that world peace essay contest in grade ten, which of course you all know about and have already read, that almost won the contest but ended up getting me suspended instead. Gave me a month or two of fame, in my school anyway. That was my first fifteen minutes, but you want to know how it became an eternity, and so here you are.

I.

SEEING'S HOW I'M all hell-bent on bending the trajectory of my life into such a different shape, you probably think I'd start by quitting smoking. At the very least switch to vaping like every other hipster and his equally annoying dog, but nope, no way no how. I love smoking and I refuse to carry that stupid box around. Like it's the same thing. And I'm not going to have to worry about cancer for long anyway. The money, fine, that's an issue, but that's another boring life's-too-short annoyance that'll happily sort itself in time too. Just got to bridge my now to your then. And tell me, what the hell-all else am I going to do with my fifteen-minute breaks?

So I'm up on C Deck and there he is again. He-who-can't-be-gotten-rid-of-lately, again. Him. Geezer's leaning over the railing and tell me if he isn't thinking of jumping. I mean, aren't we all, ultimately? Hoping to make a splash at least, at last? For him it would be a late one. But better than no splash at all? It's super calm and he's come up here what for, air? The great beyond? The beyond beyond that?

I sit near the rear of the area so he can't see me, and I light my smoke and watch him. He doesn't move. Stiff and still as the steel rail he is. His grey and black hairs sit on his head as if disappointed with the lack of wind, unimaginative dancers ensconced in silence and wishing for music but lacking the ability to imagine their own.

Wow. Look at me go. Not that that's really that good. Wind is not music, and my coding has to be more precise than that. But tell me, because I do want to know, if I can manufacture a perfect metaphor, will I be a writer? But whatever, the only writer I care about being is the useful kind—never mind saying something is *like* something, I want to make something *be* something. And then I'm going to make a lot of things be something. And what that something is is content and happy, and what those lots of things are is people. Psychopaths perhaps, *probably*, but happy's happy, and like mom and people like her are so fond of saying, let he who's without sin take me and wed me and bed me.

He's still just standing there staring out. Yes, fine, it's not odd for someone to stand at a ship's railing and stare out at an ocean, stare into the ocean of themselves, especially when the sun's summoning twinkling scallops that glisten in your squinting eyes as if there's nothing but sweet twinkly niceness in the wide world. Like someone said, land is the secure ground of home, the sea is the outside, the unknown, possibility and adventure. But the way he's standing *is* odd. Almost like he's in a crowd, pushed up against a fence with nowhere to escape to. But there's not even me as far as he knows. Again a sense that he's going to jump, like he's being forced over. If he does jump it's not like I'll have to jump into the cold water to save him, because he'll just be lying there moaning with a broken old-man bone or seventeen on the deck below like a dumb old idiot who can't judge a trajectory. But still. These days suicide's on the rise. I know this because it's another thing I've looked up. Why would he be one of the few that isn't at least tossing it over now and then?

And just in case you read that to mean *I* am too, don't you worry about me. I'm stronger than you think. I don't even cry anymore. Sure, just this morning I woke from my *dream* of crying, that one where I gush and gush uncontrollably, eyes twin spigots, releasing like a long-held piss. But even that dream-crying, it's not so much about sadness, but worry. So yeah, don't worry about me. Strong, I indeed am. But you already know this.

I guess what's most odd is my noticing him. What the hell do I care?

He shifts his weight to another foot, adjusts his lean, and now I see that what's in his hand is a bottle. A green mickey of something. Not even a mickey, smaller. A message in it? Suicide note? They'll retrieve his waterlogged cadaver and wonder why he did it, and months later, years later, the barnacled bottle'll wash up on shore in Syria or some other serious somewhere like that and it'll explain that he did himself in because he's got cancer of the does-it-even-matter and refuses to let it beat him. And the last thing anyone in that serious somewhere is going to give is a shit, so don't do it man!

Jesus, tell me what I'm doing working this damn job as a bartender on a fucking ceaselessly backtracking ferry, getting nowhere, serving drinks to why-don't-you-just-fuck-off tourists and gloomy-Gus geezers like this when I've got my app to build? My app that's going to save old geezers like this, not to mention me. Which is why you're even here!

Thinking about it counts as working on it so here's how it's going to go, once I know how to do it: Yes Paul, I'm a sheepy shmuck, an idle idiot with nothing to live for, vilest gnat alive, so yes, Paul, I'm going to do it.

But Pauline, do you not see? You deny yourself pleasure, you follow rules, you tell yourself your thoughts are bad, but why? Who do you owe? Have you not taken the lesson of modern leaders? That the idea of right and wrong has evolved? That the ideas of morality, and even personality, personhood, have moved on? How can you fail to see that the only 'wrong' is what you get caught for? And even then, if you handle it right, you're not wrong for long.

Paul, I appreciate your trouble here, I do, but your words seem to just throw into sharper relief the fact that I don't deserve to live.

What? You crazy! What do you mean deserve? No one deserves to live! And no one deserves to not live. We just are. You need to start thinking about numero uno, you know? Drink! Smoke! Be merry! Fuck people. Hark, please! Cease and desist with the harping, Carpe Diem! Who's to say what shit's wrong? You think people really care? Look at the world! Partake and take your part, whatever you can get! Those people know rules are written only for those who get comfort from following them. And to prosecute the powerless. Those who haven't risen above them. Go get high and fuck and eat and go skydiving, rinse and repeat!

If I live ugly like that, I deserve to live even less than that.

Get it through that dense braincase, there is no deserve to live. Maybe if you don't have the balls to go and take and risk stepping on toes, then perhaps. Think about 7.5 billion people on this planet, think about ten, and think about the one-percent—that's a nice refreshingly small number isn't it? Wouldn't it be nice to imagine the planet green again, with only one-one-hundredth of the people on it? Sure, maybe the population is set to start falling in fifty years, but that's still a truck-full of fucking people. These people want their genes to be part of that one percent that makes it, that come out the other side of the great die-off that's coming, and when it's only them, no one of them is going to be thinking of those stupid sheepy schleps they stepped on. If this modern world doesn't demonstrate that religious ideals and morality are dead and gone as you get, well, not sure even I can help you there, mate! When it's a matter of survival, morals are a waste of space. And it's always a matter of survival.

Well, that may be a shitty, non-researched, non-genius and wholly only-me version of my *Pep Talk Paul* app, maybe even *ugly,* but the point is once it's built and big as Facebook, *taken over* Facebook with its surrounding ecosystem, guys like this grey-haired sad-ass won't have to wallow in their own pitiful self-condemnation and hatred anymore because they'll have my AI Paul, their perfect-fit-best-ever-friend, that they can talk to to help them resolve shit, help them see that only the weak give up, that… well, I don't know exactly—that's what the app's going to do! Have you read anything at all about the potential of AI? And I'm six months into my own study and now two months into my online coding course and I'm well on my merry way. And even I can't imagine the real possibilities! And it's not the finished product that matters, it's the idea, and once I've got the basics down and have a version that demonstrates the potential, you wait and see how you'll have to hold back the fucking Brins and Zucks and Bezoses who'll be chucking seriously big bucks at me. And you'll be welcome (you are!).

Shit! I'm five minutes over my break! Clair's gonna freak!

2.

"You know, I've been ignoring you rumming up your Pepsis all week. Seeing's how I could get fired for that, and me fired because of you is not something you want to see, you might think about at least tipping me the socially accepted rate." This is me. Trying to be this kind of person.

"Well, I…"

Tell me if he's thrown by my calling him out on the booze or for being cheap, because I don't know. He doesn't seem like he's got much reason to care about either.

"I'm on a bit of a… fixed income."

"Ah." *Ah*. "My grandmother refers to it as an income in need of fixing."

He gives me a big, white, dentury smile. He should stick with the half ones he's been giving me till now, because this really brings out his wrinkles.

He's been on almost every one of my crossings the last two weeks, which is very strange. Yes, there are delivery guys, Canada Post and UPS and such, whose routes align with my shifts, and I see them regularly, but this guy's not that. And he's always writing away in a notebook, so maybe he's a wannabe writer or something, hoping to finally break big time by writing his big idea about… a bartender on a Newfie fucking ferryboat? More likely he's another terrorist researching a way to blow up this rust-bucket and punch his ticket to paradise by writing the end of our stories for us. Prefers his women wrapped up and ready to be stuck. But they're not allowed to drink, right? Or maybe he's stalking me. Ha! Yeah, *right*. I was probably right with thinking he's just working up the balls to jump ship on his life by jumping off this one.

"So what's a fixed-incomer doing riding this ferry back and forth? Don't you like to actually get places? Taking the whole journey-not-the-destination thing a little far, aren't you?" Nothing. "Where do you sleep?"

"You know that Airbnb thing?" he says finally, with his weird accent.

"Yeah." Not that I've ever used it. Probably wouldn't even ever get off the damn Rock if it wasn't for this job.

"I stay in one of those in Sydney, but in Port aux Basques, I stay in a hotel. Well, more of a motel."

"How long you plan on doing this?"

"Till I get where I'm going, I suppose."

He says this with another big smile, like he thinks he's being cute or funny or something. Let's see how funny he finds it when they come and arrest him for suspected terroristic activities. When *I* report him. It is part of my job, after all. He doesn't look Muslim exactly, but he definitely isn't from Sweden.

"Why?" I hear myself say, the word I promised myself I wouldn't use anymore. But it's not like any promise I've ever made has made my life any better. Not that there are many I've kept, I guess, so tell me what I know.

"I'd rather not say."

"Because you don't want to have to kill me?"

"No, no. I'd just be embarrassed."

3

So I brought him home. Offered and he accepted. Like an abandoned dog or something, hopped in my car and came with me to my sombre subterranean corner of Corner Brook, and what of it? Glass houses, my mom was big on saying too. Because she was all glass, believe you me. This geezer, I don't know, but right now he looks every bit the old man who's found himself sitting on a musty old sofa in a damp basement apartment belonging to the unattractive girl that's been serving him spiritless Pepsi the last three weeks. Which is to say he looks like a fish out of his school, a fish trying to ride a bicycle he got as a present from his estranged dad he almost never sees. Who didn't even hang around long enough to even give him a lesson.

He takes a long sip of his beer. Wish I had some near-beer to give him for a laugh maybe.

Weird how hard it is to tell how old he is. He's not too wrinkled, when he's not giving his fake-toothy too-big smile, anyway. His hair's thick and full but way more salt than pepper, his too-close-together hazel eyes clear as a two-year-old's conscience. His face is perfectly shaved every day, though that's obviously a job that's sent many blades to early graves. His skin's almost *blue*. Weird, with beards so popular right now—especially for old geezers such as this one. I read that men in Iran or somewhere like that over there are getting pubic hair implanted into their faces. Tell me, please, because I need to know, WTF? And men say *we're* bad. Maybe I should do some good! Get a permanent Brazilian and donate some of my surfeit of follicles! But those weirdos believing masculinity boils down to hair probably don't want *Christian* pubes on their faces. Though if you haven't been to church since you were seven, and the only time God comes out of your mouth is when it's attached to *damn* or *please*, are you still Christian?

Maybe he just likes the feel of the smooth to rough over the course of the day, how it marks time—like how my curls flatten out over my shift, so when I look my ugliest at least I know it's almost over.

"Not much of a conversationalist, are you?" I try. Stating the obvious has long been a forte of mine, and fortes aren't exactly my forte, so…

"Not these days so much."

"Why's that?"

"I suppose it's the shortage of happy endings."

"Better than sitting there in silence."

"You sure?"

Jesus, where are all the normal people you hear so much about? The *happy* people? They exist, don't they? Well, they will when Paul's available! "How old *are* you, exactly?"

"Too old for you."

Maybe if I had better legs.

"Fuck this," I say, and tell me is there a more rewarding pair of words to utter defiantly, other than maybe *take that!* which I unfortunately have never had the occasion to use other than when playing first-person shooter video games with my jerk-bag ex who was obsessed with such shit. And what else do you say when you've decided to break out your stash of pills. You were going to quit for good, you told yourself, but seeing's how you kept some, for *emergencies,* you must have meant later. And three months is a long time and deserves celebrating. And now that you think about it, three months of having them around and not needing them enough to use them really *does* deserve celebrating.

"What's this?" he asks.

"Arthritis pills. Go on, try one. Maybe you'll find a happy ending."

"Arthritis pills."

"Take your mind off it, at least."

Tell him to look at me with a you-think-because-you're-young-you-know-more-about-drugs-than-I-do? look, and then pull out a stash of some exotic something I've never had and will never need anything other than, but he doesn't. He's just a man looking at me blankly. Which, truth be told, if it fucking has to be, is not newsworthy.

"Go on. You don't really want to be any length of time in a basement apartment with someone on speed unless you're on it too." I pop mine, and he's a too-old kid watching a magic show, convinced the miracle's in the gears and no miracle at all. "Someone your age really worried about blowing a mental gasket or whatever?"

"Well, my heart's not…" A look comes over him that I bet there are people out there who could translate into words, Margaret Atwood or Adele or someone, but not me. He holds his upturned hand out, and I put two in there, then take one back, seeing's how the last thing I need on my hands is an old man flying downhill with no brakes.

"Because," he says, "I retired six months ago and I'm at wit's end and it's time to go out and live my life while there's still some left and ever since I was sixteen I wanted to be a sailor and I tried to join the navy but because of my glasses I was rejected and had to join the army and go and live and train in the blinding desert sun, getting sand in my eyes, the sand and the sun and the dry making my vision worse and grinding my nose in the fact that I was as far from the sea as one can be. I sure got my wet when I went to Vietnam, though. I'd just come to Canada and it wasn't in that war, but by that point America was taking anyone fit and willing so I caught the bus to Buffalo and signed up. I was born too late to fight Franco, so here was my chance to finally go at some communists. But it was the wrong kind of wet, land wet, humid and sucking breathy wet as hell… blood wet, the wet of freshly dead…" He looks around, like coming up out of a hole. "Where was I?"

"I asked you why you're riding a ferry back and forth across a channel."

"Because I've never felt content in my life and I've covered enough land in my taxi to last a lifetime and now I deserve to do something for myself since I've got no one else to do anything for so there, *there* I am, on your ferry, a sailor in my own mind. And I'll do this until I run out of money for good, and if I'm not dead yet I'll just set off on a walk along the coastline and it'll become a crawl and I'll just keep going, pretending I'm ship-wrecked and washed up on the shores of paradise, and hopefully my exhaustion will result in a delusion that will seem real and I'll die there and be fine, as long as I'm in sand that's ocean wet."

Boy is it fun to watch people do speed for the first time! "Holy shit!" I say and laugh. "You're the master of long sentences!" He just looks at me with his too-close-together eyes. "And I sure hope it's summer when you run out of money!"

"What do you know about long sentences?" he says with one of those looks that make you think someone's going to laugh, but then they don't and you'd better think of something fast because good god don't you start fucking crying on me.

"Just *relax*," I tell him, and he says he is but he isn't.

"Kind of hard with whatever it is you've given me."

"Yeah, it *should* be hard. You've got to relax."

I mess around a little longer with his soggy slug, a barely filled water balloon, and tell me I'm not heroic for trying to imagine it's a dead baby I'm resurrecting. But it's just limp dead flesh, deader than dead, because at least dead flesh gets stiff eventually, has some backbone.

He pushes away, and I let him. God damn it.

"No offense," he says.

Which I don't take offense to, because I well know fat-and-flat's no one's type, and no porn's gonna sell that's got thighs like mine in it.

And now tell me, what do I do now? Did I really invite him over for sex? Sometimes I feel like a bicycle with its front wheel missing. Am I really helping myself by trying to stick any warped old thing between my forks? But there *is* something about him. Like, he's not that bad looking; some George Cloonyness to him. Or maybe I'm as desperate as I'm no doubt seeming to you.

"He's yours?" he says now, and it takes me a minute to figure. Fuck.

"No, the fucking photo came with the fucking frame," says I.

"Is this an old picture?"

"He's four the end of December."

"And he…" His beard's growing in bluer.

"They took him. He's a fucking *ward* of the government. You know? All those lying dicks? They're his parents. Basically the damn queen of England. I get the privilege of visiting him three times a year. Which you might want to call pretty fucking sad. Queen Elizabeth's kid now, but he isn't on the cover of *Hello!* and he doesn't live in fucking Buckingham, either."

"Probably not in a basement, though," says this old geezer with dick of dough but balls of steel. And I guess he's probably right.

"Do you have any fucking kids?" I say, harsher than I wanted, but what's he expect with the way he's talking?

"Why did he get taken away?"

"I said do *you* have any kids?" Not that a *man* is ever going to truly understand. How could they? And isn't that the root of the whole damn problem?

"One." Something in his eyes says he's lying. "Why did they take yours?"

"Have a guess," I tell him, and you might think he'd be scared to, but he says he guesses I just wasn't ready to be a mother.

He's looking at me like I'm some stubby girl the age of his granddaughter who just tried to give him oral sex and who he didn't push away until it was obvious he was only doing it because he was never going to get it up.

"So, that explains that," he says, pointing to the heap of sleepers in the corner.

I pull my quilt tighter over my legs, and he looks at it, then gives me a look like a father would give his kid if something didn't need saying. Which is to say that's a big *if* said sad-ass father actually knew what things not to say instead of saying every god damn thing that passed through his stupid testosterone-steeped brain that you can't believe is the supposed culmination of billions of years of evolution.

He gets up and goes over to the sleepers, picks one up, examines the borders of the hole in the chest. "What are you going to do with them? Just throw them away?"

"You have any idea how you feel about these things? Once you've lost your kid? The ones he didn't even get to outgrow?" Tell me how it feels like a skin. Tell me how when he's taken from you, this is all you have left to feel? "Empty fucking hugs."

"My mother," he says, "when I was growing up, she used to make extra money selling her embroidery in Santiago's shade on Sundays. She used to… I'm just asking what you're going to do with these."

"Well, I can't throw them away. Guess I was probably just going to stick them in a garbage bag and bury them in the closet for me to find years later and lose my shit over."

"Let's fix them up." He's on his feet. He's full of energy. His sentences are normal length again.

"What?"

"You ever hear that a net is a collection of holes tied together with string?"

"Huh?"

"I mean, we're high on your drug and in need of something to do anyway. Let's patch up the holes and then… I don't know, donate them or something."

"Patch them?"

"Happy endings! Maybe someday in the future you'll see some mother with her baby wearing one of these, and you'll smile, thinking of how… how at least that one's hugs aren't empty anymore."

I look at him like he's crazy because how else am I supposed to look at this growing-somewhat-attractive old man suggesting we spend the night fixing the holes I've made in things?

"In the army we had to mend our own clothes. Had a sewing kit and everything. I actually enjoyed it. Making whole, perfect enough again. Reminded me of my mother, you know?"

I once read about erections. I'm no perv and as a girl I think it's normal to be amazed by them, seeing's how this limp thing becomes hard so it can force its way in through way too softly defended gates and shoot spermatozoas at our eggs, all to make new people. And now, this doughy-dicked old man, talking about his mother who made him and about patching up holes in sleepers I've ruined to make a quilt that only leaves me colder. I remember the first time I tried patching up my bike tire. Five fucking times I tried and it just got flatter. Holier and holier.

A collection of holes. Sounds like people in general.

"All right then," I say. "Maybe you can sell them and fix your income a little bit."

4.

BOY IT'S A shit day out there. Try and tell water from fog. No matter the clarity above, though, what lies beneath is never seen. I'm not afraid of the deep end, but if you find out too much and then proceed to overthink said too much you've learned about what's underneath, well... Like: the Cabot Strait, with the Laurentian Channel cutting a deep gash through its centre, has a max depth of five-hundred-fifty metres. Half a damn kilometre of water, a cubic metre of which weighs a tonne, so find yourself at the bottom of this strait that this ferry service has supposedly been traversing since 1898 and you've got five-hundred tonnes of water weighing you down in salty depths no light's ever gonna reach, never mind a search party. But never even mind that: follow that channel two hundred nautical miles southeast and it's a sheer drop off the continental shelf into the Sohm Abyssal Plain (if I ever find myself in a band this is going to be its name!) and the ocean floor proper. *Six kilometres* below. In my training course I put my hand up and asked what's the deepest ocean in the world and they told me The Marianas Trench, which I'd heard of, is ten kilometers deep. I looked it up and its depth is actually *eleven* clicks (and there is a band named that!)—you could stick Everest at the bottom of that and drop ocean levels two kilometres and Everest's peak still wouldn't even tear the bottom out of Titanic. Which, the trainer mentioned, sank just southeast of Newfoundland, but anyone who grows up in Newfoundland grows up knowing that, seeing's how we don't have all that much to be famous for.

But the ocean's scary depths only add weight to the terror of the things that take place on its surface, which our trainer turned to next. The Channel's depth is very varied, and so supposedly this creates a high likelihood of rogue waves in the area.

It's a super dangerous area, supposedly, the Grand Banks being prone to crazy vicious storms that come on fast and have claimed the lives of a fair few shivering fisherman. Trainer told us to read The Perfect Storm for a better idea and I did and damn, I used to think drowning would be one of the best ways to go, but after reading that book I think I'd rather be tied upside down over a pyre and burned head first (like you know some especially gleeful outside-the-box burners of witches did from time to time). And they told us about St. Paul Island, marking the hard right off the Gulf of St Lawrence into the Cabot Strait, and how it's supposedly named the Graveyard of the Gulf because it's often fogbound and lots of ships sank around it. When I'm taking a break up top and looking North I think of it up there, and I think about the fact that if all of a sudden, or even all of a gradual, this ship below me cracked in half and I found myself in the cold wet tumult being sucked down and holding and holding and holding my breath until I couldn't anymore and inhaling a fiery gulp of fatal saltwater into my lungs, I'd be just a mundane 'nother notch on the belt of the ocean's battle against individuals.

Course the whole lot of us together are giving the ocean overall a good bludgeoning, so guess joke's on it. *Take that.*

Imagine being on a ship alone out there. In the middle of the real ocean? Imagine becalmed in a pea soup fog, not even the slightest wave lapping at the hull. An ocean of stillness. Imagine, needing to conserve your batteries so not even playing your music. And you're too far from land for there to be any life in the skies, and there's nothing moving. You've even brought your sails down because they're just hanging there like a dress, making you mad with their silence. Imagine the still static nothing, how scary it would be. How convinced you'd be something really bad was lurking below.

Fuck, I feel like I'm almost having an anxiety attack. Haven't felt this in a while. Three months. The low after the high. Why did I do it? Why did I invite him over? Something about him, fine. Something about anyone. But why the speed?

But, tons of people use that. Loads of Asians, for sure. All that pressure to study and work all the time, and tell me they're not doing pretty well for it. They're taking over the world! Point being, a lot of people use a lot of drugs to get a lot of shit done, and I've got shit I've got to get done speedily. Lots of wrongs to right. I'm three days behind now on my coding course thanks to bringing James over and his speed-fuelled fucking sewfest and bringing those sleepers in to donate them. I wonder if they actually put them on the racks. God, tell me they didn't just chuck them in a cruddy dumpster because I'm not sure I could live with myself if I have to picture them rotting in a stench-strangled landfill some desolate nowhere. Why did I let him convince me to do that? Because the speed, that's why. Gotta quit that shit for good. Pretty sure Sergei and Zuck steer clear of that shit. My generation's supposed to be post-drugs. We're supposed to be cleaner than that. Better. Smarter. Right? Whatever, none of that's going to matter once Pep Talk Paul's done and up and running and I'm shopping my miracle code around and choosing the biggest bunch of billions. I'll hire and buy whatever and whoever the hell I need to get shit done and get Alex back and be the best fucking mother any family court judge ever done did see.

Wonder what Captain Stitch is up to. Is he on my alter ego ferry? On his way to Porto, or is he taking the day off in his little room? Is he out for a walk. Is he writing whatever he's writing? Did he have a heart attack from the speed? Did he go crazy from it? Set off on his walk along the coastline?

Why do I care? Tell me what the fuck?

Paul?

5.

"I DROPPED SOME stuff off last week, and I can't find it anywhere," I tell her, trying to ignore how barely she looks at me.
But still, how hard is it to interact pleasantly with people you're
basically paid to do that very thing with? One thing about me, I
know how to fake fucking nice when I have to.

"Why are you looking to buy what you dropped off?" she
asks, like I'm probably some auditor trying to catch her out for
stealing donations. I wonder if they have such people. Which
they probably should.

"Because obviously I thought someone might need them,
and I was hoping to see them on frigging hangers, which is something I don't."

"We only put things of a passable quality on the floor," she
says. "I'm sure you can understand that a lot of people use us as
a free version of the dump."

F-F-FU— "Seeing's how," I say, calmly, remembering how
Alex's dolt dad did just what she is saying, even after I told him
no one would want his shit and he knew it but he 'donated' it
anyway. "But…" I can't think of anything else. It's true, they're
junk. These days, with clothes so cheap, they were just patched
up junk. I ruined them all.

A memory of Alex comes to mind, in the blue sleeper with
the white bicycle silhouettes, his arms reaching out to me, his legs
cycling, his lips bent into a perfect smile. His perfect laugh. His
perfect fucking everything. Except mother and father.

He's loving someone else now. Bruce and Fran–fucking–cine.
But he's loving?

"Maybe they got all bought already," she offers.

I go back and flick through the hangers again, wondering
where all the babies who wore these are now, and wondering

about their mothers and wondering about their fathers, and if they even ever held these.

I don't find them. Not a one. There are lots of others, but none of mine. None with holes, fixed or not. I press on. Into the two-year-old section because maybe they've been misplaced because people who shop charity shops aren't the type to give a shit about putting things back where they got them—if they'd been able to get such lesson through their dense braincases they probably would have gotten other lessons as well and not ended up sliding hangers along the chrome poles of charity stores' stale offerings and BAM! I FIND ONE!! I FUCKING FIND ONE! THE OTHERS SOLD BECAUSE THEY HAVE WORTH AND ARE SELLABLE! THE PATCHES MAKE THEM THAT MUCH MORE *Wait* a second. There's no patch on this. It's brand-fucking-new. Fuck. Of course it is! Like I was buying one-offs designed just for my precious that no one else anywhere in the world would be able to have a version of. Like mine were anything other than dime-a-dozen made-by-slave-labour with crap fabrics and cheap cheesy designs. And who the fuck donated this brand new one? Some rich bitch who didn't even need it. Some... Wait though. Maybe it's some sad-ass mother, infinitely sadder than me mother, whose baby died. Some mother whose baby died of SIDS or whatever before even having a chance to wear this sleeper that someone she loved gave to her as a gift, and that she received with smiles and laughs that can never be had again because she at that time when her baby was alive and kicking and smiling was on top of her world and experiencing universal highs of quantum connection to systems that are all linked and interrelated and there for one another. And then he died. And so did she. But not before suffering pain greater than any bitch witch burned head-first.

I think of my Alex, alive and breathing out there, and I try to be grateful, and I am. I really am, even if there's a massive fucking BUT to it. So be it. And God grant me the serenity to accept the things I cannot change. But if you're feeling generous tonight, with your endless power feel free to go ahead and rebirth me in a world devoid of all this shit.

—

It's cold and it's damp and it's half-assed raining, and driving home I crank the heat because I want to feel hot and comfortable yesterday and I can't bear to go home right now and my crappy old Corolla hasn't even warmed me by the time I get there so I keep on going. I think of going to see my mom but that would be dumb. I think of Tika, but she'll be working right now. She's a teacher. And she has two kids who are doing well because their dad's a decent man with a decent job as a cop and so going to see them would be even more stupid.

Tell me, cause I want to know, am I just jealous?

It's natural human nature to feel a bit of resentment for those who have it better than you do when you are not where you want to be. Nothing wrong with that. It's biological. Motivates and stimulates. Competition. Get those genes through to the next generation, you know? Name of the game! And it's not like you want her to lose every-thing she has.

Well, no, not *everything.* No children need die or be stolen. But surely there's a happy middle ground (You have to be super honest with Paul for him to work properly (which is what's going to make him ultimately so valuable. Think of the data!)).

So the best text you hope to get right now is one from her with a wailing emoticon followed by the flaming mad face and the words I just found out fucking Matt has been fucking Jane every third fucking night! *No, you don't want that. You admit to yourself you think you do, but you don't. Because you know what's better for you than that is for you to not want to feel and be better because others are brought down relative to you, but to feel and be better objectively, to* join *the happy, not make them all sad-asses. You're in it tough right now, but you're going to be world famous, the most famous by far to come out of Corner Brook. Allison Crowe'll know who you are! And this is going to change the world. And Alex will be back under your warming wing, under your sky-high skylight-strewn roof.*

I know, Pep Talk Paul's too much talk not enough pep right now, isn't he? Not exactly going to turn a deep-depressive Denise into a sunshine-spewing Sally, but you might think about the fact that this is just me trying my best, while driving, without even the help of a famous quote. So it's not bad for that, and the proof's in the pudding because I do feel better. And I'm finally warm. In fact, I have to turn the heat down. And don't you hate that? You get into a car freezing and you crank the heat and know that before long all will be well and right and toasty, all your troubles sweetly behind you, and you can't wait, and then it starts to come, and it's wonderful, but so quickly it switches to too hot, and you have to turn it down, and you're okay, but there's nothing to be excited about anymore. I don't turn it down. I try to dwell, revel in it and appreciate it. I try to imagine myself cold, freezing fuck cold, freezing to death and imagining this. But now I'm sweating and I have to turn it off. And now I have to open the damn window.

I'm passing by the Marble Inn resort and I consider renting some skis and going skiing but I'm too tired, and I'll just be cold again. So I keep on driving. And I hear Paul: *I don't mean to be a pain, but you should probably get home and get to work on your courses. I'm not going to write myself, now am I? Ha!*

And he's right. Damn right. As he's always going to be. So I turn around and decide that I'm going straight home and I'm going to put in at least five hours today, and another five tomorrow. And I'm going to add another five pages to my database of quotes. These ones'll be on jealousy. The ugliest of uglies.

And then work on Monday and tell me 'cause I guess I want to know, but please don't tell me I care: will my geezer be aboard?

6.

"It's on me tonight," I say, pouring a shot for myself and giving his glass a knock. God, I hate hard stuff, but this wannabe sailor's gotta drink what sailors've supposedly gotta drink, I guess.

I do a round of the tables, get no orders, and go back to him at the bar. Yes, he's at the bar this time, for some reason, like it's his obligation now I've had his disfunction in my mouth, and I'm a bit annoyed, but only a bit, which is probably pretty problematical.

"I'm choosing to go with the idea that they all got sold already," I tell him. "That people saw those patches and felt the love. Plus, they were probably cheaper than the perfect ones."

He gives me a new kind of smile I haven't seen yet. "I should be buying you drinks."

"Tell me who's stopping you."

"I told you I went to Vietnam?"

And how. Felt the age difference then, let me tell you. A soul difference. "Oh boy, here we go." Although, tell me, are we not all searching for something we'd kill for?

"We got separated from our unit. Lost. And Oz was shot. In the side. I sewed him up, really close, tight stitches, and I carried him until I couldn't go any further, and then I stopped and we slept. Or so I thought. When I woke up he was gone. My stitches had opened. I'd put too many in and the skin ripped apart, and he'd bled out. He was stiff and white, empty and gone."

"Shit."

"To say the least."

"And so patching up those sleepers…"

He looks at me, dark eyes like holes. "Well, you seem patched up a little bit, at least."

And tell me if it's true, cause I want to know.

No, it's not fucking true. And I don't need patching up anyway. "I'm fine and I've been fine. The trick is to have a plan."

He nods. "So you have a plan?"

"I figure two years and I'll be ready."

"What's that then?"

"You know what coding is?"

"You mean computer programming."

"I'm taking online courses and learning how to do it. It's not that hard, really. Just tedious. Takes time and attention."

"That's good. But won't you miss the sea?" He says this with a wink, as if he thinks I hate it. Like I don't have it in me to love it. Like he doesn't know you can't be capable of hate without being capable of love.

"For your information I actually would, but I won't have to because I'll have it in a whole new way. Any way I want. I'm not going to be a programmer. I have an idea for an app. An *application*, you know? I won't even have to go all the way to making a start-up and all that. I don't care about having a business. God, I think I'd die if I had to go to one of those expos to pitch to investors in ten seconds or less. I'm just going to write this app, the basics anyway, and then I'll sell it. For a lot."

"A plan and a half. What's it going to do?"

"I can't tell you."

"Because you don't want to have to kill me?"

"Exactly right old man. But I'll tell you the name. It's called Pep Talk Paul. And yes, it's going to sell for lots. You can't even imagine. Fucking I barely can."

"But you can."

"One thing I'm going to get is a yacht with its own private beach. Would you believe they actually have those now? And it'll hurt my finances like a normal person buying a rubber dinghy. Hell, a rubber duck."

"Good to have goals."

If he weren't so old, a bit more wized up, he'd be telling me it's a pipe dream, that everyone and their dog's dog's fleas've got an idea for an app that's going to make them gajillions. Guess this geezer doesn't know enough about the modern world to even know that. Look at him, writing with a fucking wood pencil that he sharpens with a black Swiss army knife. Into a notebook. Slowly, like every letter matters, like he has all the time in the world. Like he doesn't even want to get where he's going. Like he doesn't know he's there already.

"You know, James, if you really value what you're writing, you might want to get a laptop to type into. You lose that notebook and it's gone forever. They're not even expensive. Not to mention pencil fades, you know."

He gives me a little grin, one I haven't seen before, one that better not signify that he's about to say something to make me feel like a kid.

"This writing, Pauline, it's more like therapy. Like bailing out a boat. I don't want the words to last. I just need to get them out. I tear out the pages and burn them every night."

"Like Buddhists with their sand art stuff."

"More like, removing a cancerous tumour."

"Well…"

"Yeah."

Clair's fine with it so I take a smoke break and James comes with. There's no one else on top deck and it's cold and it's windy and we cross the blue rubber matting to the railing, but I can't get my smoke lit so we move up to the shelter behind the captain's bridge. Which today is Steve and he's an asshole, so I make sure I'm in the corner so he can't see me. Cigarette lit, I take a couple long hauls and James is looking out at the sea with the look of one hoping for a rogue wave—whether to surf or be washed away by is not clear. You get the feeling probably it never is for him. Which must be pretty problematical.

"I had a limited success at real writing," I hear myself tell him for some reason. Probably just to say something, but probably also taking a rare opportunity to brag about something. "The only success I've ever had at anything, actually, other than getting accidentally knocked up."

"Yeah?"

"Highschool writing contest. Theme was world peace, of course. It was supposed to be an essay but that was ass-boring so I wrote a story about a penis enlargement technique that's discovered to actually work. A combination of baking soda, you know, makes shit rise, soil from the grave of someone who died in 1919, just to be obscure, bicycle chain oil, can't remember my thinking on that one, and then meditating whenever possible on horses fucking, you know, envisioning success."

"Funny," he says, without actually laughing, of course.

"So guys go crazy for it, and over the next few months they're all engaged in a kind of arms race, what was big last week isn't anymore, and now no women will have sex with them because they're too big and we're finally and forever turned off by such a proving of how embarrassingly vain, dumb and competitive men are, and so the number of rapes goes through the roof but then suddenly all the men become intellectually stunted because all the blood's going to their member and not their brain and they all have to be put in facilities where they're given all the food and beer and porn they can consume, and they all just turn gay and eventually they all die from their injuries. And there's peace at last."

He's looking at me like I mean something a little different now.

"School had a bit of a problem with it, so I got suspended. My gay English teacher loved it, though, said it was hilarious, *brilliant* satire. So feminist. Said I had talent. And he was even published himself. I put it out there by Facebook and it gave me a name for a while, but not enough to be actually accepted. In fact most people labelled me more of a freak afterwards—it's not like I'd written a story about an uber cool sexy clique of teenage wizards or vampires or shit like that."

"Wow, well…"

"I tried another one, about a psychopath who feels no empathy, though he's heard about it and knows what it is so he's intrigued by it, but not in a caring way, in a what-a-weird-thing-how-neat way. He seeks it out and studies Christianity and heaven and hell and is right terrified of burning forever so he decides to be good but knows doing it for only selfish reasons is never going to actually cut it, so, feeling barred from heaven forever he goes mad and decides to at least properly deserve his hell-fires so he sets off on a killing spree, wondering if maybe the devil will be impressed and hire him on instead of torturing him."

"You're kidding."

"Nope. Teach liked that one too, though he said it was way too heavy-handed and sentimental."

We sit quiet for a while and I'm somehow disappointed he doesn't have more to say. Don't try and get more than fifteen minutes from your fifteen minutes, is I guess the point.

"Have you ever heard of the Vendée Globe?" he says finally, I guess to offer something of himself, or just to keep the conversation going. "It's a sailing race around the world unassisted and alone. All the way around. First one to do it took ten months, but these days it takes about three for the fastest ones. Four or five for the slowest."

"Sounds dangerous as hell."

"People have died in it. In fact, it's probably the most dangerous major sporting event ever held if you look at the percentage of participants who have died. Other than bull-fighting, anyway. They sail straight down the Atlantic then under Africa and across and under down under and then South America. Basically a circumnavigation of Antarctica. The most dangerous seas, most isolated place in the world. Roaring Forties and Furious Fifties. Way out of range of helicopters and no other ships around. Have trouble out there and no one's getting to you for days. One of the sailors, in sixth place right now, in the 2008 edition he broke his leg eight-hundred nautical miles off Australia and had to lie in bed in agony for two whole days before a rescue ship reached him."

"And he's doing it again?"

"Yep."

"Can't cure stupid," I say, stupidly, and feel the hairs on the back of my neck stand up. I picture myself on a boat with one of them, what it would be like to be with a man like that, a rare example of a truly manly man? "That's crazy shit."

"I started my first leg of this ferry adventure on the sixth, which is the day that they all set off. That's my timeline for this. The first sailor will likely finish well before the end of January. The rest, well, could be months before the last one's in. Someone sailing now could very well be dead. Dead this very moment... I was thinking that I'd kind of isolate myself away like they have. I'm not reading any news at all since starting this. The only news I'm reading is about that race."

I put my cigarette out in my portable ashtray and light another. The sea looks different now. The ship, so massive underneath me, feels different. "Then what? When that race is done? I thought you were doing this till you run out of money."

He hesitates, turns away from me. "Wouldn't you just love to see one of those beautiful boats sail past right now, like..." He's looking out at the blue grey, maybe imagining the fleet of them coming over the horizon, sleek and vivid and bold, a flock of exotic birds or fish, like a magic show. But there's nothing else out there. Nary a shearwater or a tern. Not even a seagull to be seen.

You don't grow up on Newfoundland without some sea and sailing in your blood. I was what, maybe ten? Who the hell brought me? I watched them sail off, on their Around The Rock race, so clean and colourful and so gracefully lively, and their contrast against the grey and blue and white was stark, but as they got further away their colour and size faded, as they were pressed between the sky and sea of the horizon, like flowers pressed to dry and die between the pages of books, like being crushed out of existence—but I knew they were still there, like the printed words in a closed book. But I also knew they weren't nearly as safe. I feared the immensity of the ever-after. But it also reassured me because absence is the absence of good things, yes, but it's also the absence of bad things. Which is ultimately totally unproblematical.

I've got to close the bar in fifteen minutes and prepare for landing, so I ask him if he'd like anything else. He'd like another Pepsi and I give it to him.

"You know," I say, putting the last of the glasses into the washer, "that race around the world. Makes me think of when I was in grade four we had this kid, my teacher's nephew or something, seemed so old but was probably only like seventeen, come and talk to the school. He had just biked across Canada. Alone. Like Terry Fox, they said, except both his legs were fine and I assume both wheels were too. For cancer he said, though he didn't have it, just said any one of us could have a cell mutating cancerously in us right this moment, which was a freaky thought. One of his PowerPoint slides was a map of Canada with us on the far end as usual and he showed his route and how far he went and how many miles every day and I was just amazed. It was the first time I realised just how big the world is, while at the same time realising that it was a complete thing, a place after a place after a place, all linked and joined back around, all out there and capable of being tackled. And on a *bike*. I mean, *I* had a *bike*. I even liked riding it. I imagined doing something like that. Just one turn of the pedal after another, a lowly one times a billion, or a trillion. And growing up here, hemmed in between a huge sea on one side and a huge sea of land on the other. Maybe I could at least ride around Newfoundland or something. I actually measured how far my bike went on one revolution of the pedals and then broke out my calculator and started playing with the biggest numbers it could handle, you know, like, one revolution per second, sixty seconds in a minute, then an hour, eight hours in a day times 365…"

He's looking at with me with the most interest yet. "And?"

"I went for a long bike ride that Saturday, all one way, and had no energy to get back and had to call my mother to come and get me in her boyfriend's beater truck and we got a flat tire and she had to change it, cursing the whole time. She grounded me from my bike for the rest of summer. Popped the tires to be sure."

"The most famous sailor in the first Vendée, The Golden Globe that race was called, was this Frenchman Bernard Moitessier. Hard parts done he was sure to win, be the first in man's long history of sailing to circumnavigate the world alone non-stop and unassisted, the last sailing first left, and probably the most incredible. It was his. Just imagine. Then, halfway up the Atlantic, man decides he can't return to the modern world. He was so at peace on the sea, on his boat, he couldn't bear coming back, and so he turned around and went two thirds of the way around again. Under Africa again, once more under down under, then landed at Tahiti, almost a year after setting off. In sixty-nine. A month before we stepped on the moon for the first time. Must have felt similar for him stepping onto land."

"Serious?"

"Man was a bit of a hippie."

"So what happened?"

"A Limey won it. Robin Knox-Johnston. Military man. Only one to finish."

"What's a Limey?"

He smiles. "Term for a British person. Comes from the old days of sailing. The British used to add lemon juice to the daily ration of grog, which was watered-down rum. The vitamin C prevented scurvy."

"Hmmm… So the Frenchie let the Limey win. Crazy."

"More than you think. Another *Limey*, Donald Crowhurst, actually did go crazy and killed himself. Undid his safety tether and stepped off the stern in the middle of the Atlantic. Watched his boat sail away from him faster than he'd ever be able to swim."

7

IT'S NOT AS if he's on every one of my crossings, and he's not on this one. Not many other people, either. It's getting deeper into winter and the torrent of tourists has shrunk down to a dreggy dribble like I was told it would. I can't help but wonder where he is. Did he step off the stern and go swim for the shores of his heaven? Did last night his sleep lead him to death? Did he throw himself off a proper ledge? Did I interfere with what he had planned, what he needed to do? *Was* he planning to blow up the ship? Is it about to blow five seconds from now???

5, 4, 3, 2, 1...

What if it a bomb really *did* go off under my sad ass those seconds ago, now all of me incinerated and blown apart. Me. Gone. Gone?

Why the fucking fuck am I thinking about him so much? Seeing's how I've never had what could be classified as a *good* relationship with any man ever in my life, maybe it's that my mind has decided that an old man who can't get it up won't be able hurt me in the classical way at least.

Was I selfish? What does that message in his bottle have to say? The same things mine does?

I keep thinking what will I do if I see some mother with a baby in a sleeper with a patch on it? I'll ask why and she'll say it was the cheapest one on the rack, *duh*. Imagine buying your kid that and then seeing on a magazine cover the royal rug-rats decked out in bespoke designer clothes all neatly ironed and pressed. How fucking shit you're going to feel. And how can you not feel like those kids *are* better than yours? Intrinsically? And know *everyone* knows it? We all have to face reality sooner or later. And yet you love your kid more than yourself, and you start noticing the way people look at your kid, with pity, or even disgust. How much is that likely to turn you into a mass murderer?

That, *that right there*, is the exact moment Paul's built for!

My genes are shit. Princess Kate's fucking kid deserves air more than mine does. If there was only enough air for my boy or hers, everyone in the world would sternly stare as my sweet perfect boy gasped for breath and writhed and turned blue and finally came to an agonized still. To the relief of everyone. While the little prince licks his specialty low-fat high-taste ice cream cone and wonders what comes next.

Stop! With that attitude maybe you're right! But you're not! You're so wrong! Flip it! The royals are in-bred and everyone knows it! It's about potential!

Yes, but look at them. Their first years are already so much better. They're already so much more stimulated and well-fed. A bazillion dollars in the bank equals a lot of fucking potential duh!

No! They're just other babies. They deserve no more!

Damn it, Paul, you're wrong on this one! Clearly they're better than my child! Superior! We're not all the same!

Fine. But that's why you need to keep at it. Keep studying your code. Make me better, capable, what you have planned. So you can be there for him as soon as you can. Every child needs at least one adult who is irrationally crazy about him.

Well that was sad-ass, wasn't it? Some arguments are a lot harder to win than others.

Home now, time to get down to work! In researching PTP, which I really don't need to do that much of because once I sell it to Google or whatever they'll be able to feed it all the wisdom wise-asses and their grandmothers have ever spouted, not to mention everything they know about you and I, which is said to be likely more than even you or I know about ourselves. But I need to look like I know at least some of it, so I thought a good short cut would be to start making a database of quotes from all the ages' brainiacs of one bent or other, which I can maybe code to correlate to questions asked, so when you ask a question you get some applicable quotes to help you along. I've always loved Googling quotes, actually a bit of an addiction, because it always makes me think, and makes me feel better, *understood,* even. *Understanding?*

Imagine, an app that is all the most brilliant minds of all time made into one mind there for the sole purpose of giving you pep talks, saying things like *Some men have thousands of reasons why they cannot do what they want to do, when all they need is one reason why they can.* (That's Martha Graham, some skinny chickie who supposedly revolutionized dance more so than any other single person. She also said *The body says what words can't,* which makes me think of my old man James and what his body said to mine. But, I'm working on that, and when I've got the money, I'm going to really work on that). And then that could be followed up by a bunch of reasons to do what the person is thinking of doing, and there you go, happily and excitedly off to the races! Remember, with all the data Google and Facebook and the like has on you, they really do know the real, honest, consistent you better than even you do. And imagine how much they'll know about all of us once we all start using this app! So you're going to be powerless to disagree with Paul and his only job is to tell you what he knows you want to hear!

Speaking of what you want to hear, all of a sudden *Jackie* starts playing on my Spotify autoplay. Since I first heard it when I was thirteen, this old two-and-a-half-minute epic by Sinead O'Connor has been maybe my favourite song, and I'm instantly engulfed by the sad salty glorious defiant romance of it. The idea of a man that a woman as hard-edged and defiant and serious as Sinead O'Connor could fall so in love with. And I realise (this is me—idiot! Duh!) that what's going on here is old man James is the closest I've come to the mythic gnarly old greying sailor that I've longed for all my life. Maybe I was a sailor's wife lifetimes ago. Maybe I was a sailor myself. Hell, Noah for all I fucking knowah.

I'm not attracted to this guy, and yet, and yet… he's the closest approximation yet to a real man? This air-quotes *sailor*? And the irony, that he wanted desperately to be a sailor but couldn't be, and so here he is on my ferry demonstrating how hard-core of a sailor he actually is at his soul's root. So I don't get a real sailor, but I get a real sailor? And, don't even go there because I know, duh, I see it—he's also a father figure, which I've never fucking had, but please, save it, you don't need to tell me about how your best friend's doing her PhD in psychology and you told her about me and she told you that I'm obviously just going after this guy as a substitute for the father who did fuck all for me and might have fucked me up less if he'd actually fucked me.

  Fucking hell, *Paul!*
  You can't control the wind, but you can adjust the sail.
  Men, they're all so ugly. Near every one. Ugly. Big burly hairy *vain* and *violent* animals stalking the plain in search of things to subjugate, to subject to their sex. All ego, and what's egotism but the anaesthetic that dulls the pain of stupidity. If only this stupid triply betraying body of mine, foolish foolish body, would let me be with women I'd never go near another one again. What can I hope for? In this world, where what's held up as manliness is the opposite of what's beautiful, what's feminine, soft and gentle and loving.
  A woman knows the face of the man she loves like a sailor knows the open sea.
  Muscles and beards and money, me me me, look at glorious me. They're incapable of thinking of anyone but themselves and their own. Maybe they're just not built that way, and society strengthens that. They don't give birth, so they can't truly feel for others. Look how many of them run off on their children! And what happens to women in war—men can relate to women exactly how they want to, hating them, unless they're writhing impaled on the end of their ravenous blood-engorged swords. What do you call the fat around a vagina? A *woman.* He can fuck off. I can't do this. I need to keep on keeping on the way I know I have to. It's what I've learned. What I've been taught. Right?
  A ship is always safe at shore, but that is not what it's built for.
  Fuck, Paul! What are you even here for? On top of it all this guy's, like, *old.* Not to mention *impotent!* I don't even…

Maybe that's why you like him. He's safe. No blood engorged sword ruling him. The only man you've ever felt safe with, remember that one? was gentle, feminine, warm and giving. Gay. Isn't that how he seems? And remember, trust anyone whose boat shoes are more worn than yours.

But, I can't! I know what I need to do. I can't be distracted by this shit. I have to have control. You just fucking said! I can't control the wind, but I can adjust the sail!

The sea, once it casts its spell, holds one in its net of wonder forever. And don't forget, The Earth has music for those who listen.

You don't get it! I'm not saying I'm in love with him! I'm saying...

You want to be in love with someone. *Like the song Jackie, she died for him and he's not on the other side even but still she waits. Fine,* duh. *It's never going to be him, though. So you might as well have a friend.*

Jesus H.

8.

"THAT'S FINE. I'LL wait till you've knocked off, probably on this very ferry, then I'll just take it."

"I'm only able to do this because no one's ever going to read it."

"You're writing too much to fit in your bottle."

"What?"

"I just want to know… I don't know. You really going to make me say more than that?"

"It's not worth reading, it's not *for* reading. It's like, bailing out a boat. I'm writing out my demons, you know? Some vile bile for sure."

"But sometimes writing makes it more real."

"Could be."

"Come over tonight. I promise I won't grab at your privates."

"It won't matter to them if you do or don't."

He doesn't even wink as he says it. And tell me 'cause I need to know, is it actually excitement I feel?

We do the rest of my speed. Parts of me're relieved, like glad I've got nothing left to fall back on, but other parts of me, the most me parts of me, well, it doesn't take a rocket scientist. I think about that and for the first time ever I imagine what it would be like to have a man or a woman or a sister or a mother who could make you feel as reassured, as defended, as *safe* as a bag of speed at arm's reach.

And he's talking and talking, I guess desperate for release. He's getting sharper, more pointed, my geezer here, and I wonder if he couldn't perhaps be an exact polar opposite of my Pep-Talk-Paul. And maybe there's something in that—this world's over-populated and getting worse by the hour, maybe we need someone to convince people how shit everything is so they'll just go and blow their brains out instead of continuing to plus-up the cess in this pool.

"And you asked me if I had kids," he's saying. "Yeah I had kids. I had kids lots of damn kids. Too many. One and one too many. If you've had one you've had them all and you've had one too many and if you've lost one your mother definitely had one too many too. You try not to think about the perfection destroyed, how it seems so part of an indestructible beautiful system, one so beautiful and perfect there could be no destroying it ever because to see it destroyed would be to see a truth that was unbearable and yet people seem to survive, right? They talk about post-truth. They talk about fantasy, which never lasts. I know we all die, everything terminates, but not this, not this, this foot would never cease to be perfect and part of its system, there was no conceiving of such destruction."

And he goes on telling me and telling me and telling me, slap after stinging slap he tells at me, like some mad sad-ass rapper who's just chosen truth over money because he just this now realized how massive a scabby-ass striver dick he was making of himself, and he has to make up for it and he has the pills and the skills to pay all the fucking bills. So I demand it and he gives it to me, his notebook, which is in his sad-ass vinyl-or-some-such-cheap-depressing-as-depressing-ought-ever-be-allowed-to-get satchel, and I open it and I look at it and I look it and you might think about and fancy coming across this message bursting soggily forth from a barnacled bottle:

FUCKING I WILL FUCKING KILL YOU I NEVER DREAMED ID KILL ANYONE AND NOW I WILL KILL ANYONE AND IF I CANT HAVE YOU I WILL HAVE WHATEVER I CAN AND WILL DO IT 78 MILLION TIMES AND IT STILL WONT BALANCE AN EQUATION NEVER MIND ALL OF THEM I DON'T CARE THAT YOU HAVE A STORY BECAUSE YOU DIDN'T STOP TO THINK ABOUT HERS AND YOU WERE MADE

INHUMAN AND BE GLAD YOURE DEAD AND YOURS
ARE DEAD YOU VERMIN BECAUSE I WOULD HAVE
CAUGHT YOU AND WRAPPED YOUR HEAD IN PLAS-
TIC AND STRAPPED YOU TO A CHAIR AND NEVER
LET YOU SLEEP AND EVERY NIGHT COME BACK
AND TELL YOU ABOUT HOW I SPENT THE DAY TOR-
TURING AND KILLING ANOTHER OF YOUR LOVED
ONES AND WHEN THEY WERE ALL GONE AND IT
WAS TIME FOR ME TO FINALLY DO THE FINALE ID
HAVE SEWN YOUR EYES OPEN AND STUCK PIN
AFTER PIN INTO ONE EYE UNTIL IT WAS ALL STEEL
PIMPLES AND THEN I'D DO THE SAME WITH YOUR
SECOND EYE AND YOU'D KNOW YOU WERE NEVER
GOING TO SEE ANYTHING EVER AGAIN AND THEN
ID RIP YOUR TEETH OUT WITH PLIERS AND THEN
ID CUT YOUR TONGUE OUT BUT ID RESEARCH IT
FIRST AND MAKE SURE IT WOULDN'T RESULT IN
YOUR BLEEDING TO DEATH OR CHOKING ON
YOUR OWN BLOOD BECAUSE YOURE NOT GET-
TING OFF EVEN A TENTH THAT EASILY AND THEN
ID TAKE A HAMMER TO YOUR KNEES, AND THEN
YOUR SHINS, AND THEN TAKE ONE TESTICLE AND
CRUSH IT IN A VICE. SLOWLY. AND THEN ID TAKE
THE OTHER AND DO THE SAME. EVEN SLOWER.
AND THEN I'D TAKE AN EXACTO KNIFE AND CUT
YOUR PENIS OFF SLICE BY MILLIMETRE SLICE FROM
THE HEAD TO THE BASE SO YOU COULD FEEL IT
BEING CUT OFF A HUNDRED TIMES AND WITH A
HOT BRAND I'D CAUTERIZE EACH SLICE TO STOP
THE BLEEDING AND MAKE YOU FEEL LIKE YOU
WERE FUCKING FIRE AND BY NOW ID PROBABLY
BE TIRED AS ALL HELL AND I'D TELL YOU I HATE
HATE HATE HATE YOU AND I HOPE I SEE YOU IN
HELL WHERE IF IT'S THE LAST THING I DO I'LL DO IT
ALL AGAIN AND THEN I'D LET YOU IN ON THE
CHERRY ON TOP BY BRINGING YOUR YOUNGEST
DAUGHTER INTO THE ROOM AND LETTING HER

CRY IN YOUR EAR AND BRINGING TO YOUR DIS-
GUSTING BRAIN ALL YOUR MEMORIES OF HER AS A
BABY A PERFECT BABY AND IMAGINING EVERY-
THING SWEET AND INCORRUPTIBLE IN THE
WORLD AND HOW GOD DAMN IT WHY IS THERE
ANY SUFFERING AND IF ANYONE EVER TOUCHES
HER YOU'LL SLICE HIS THROAT AND THEN I'LL
SLICE HERS CLEANLY THROUGH AND YOU'LL HEAR
HER GURGLE BLOOD AND THRASH AND SCREAM
MAKE MECHANICAL WET WINDY SOUNDS AND
THEN—

"So, you're not quite at the forgive and forget stage," I say.

"I don't even know any more who I'm forgiving and how I
can continue to operate if I forget all the things I wish I could."

"I'm an old man and have known a great many troubles," I
hear myself say, "and some of them even happened."

He's looking at me, wondering if I'm quoting or that's me.

"Just promise me cuz I need to fucking know, you're not
actually a terrorist scoping out the ferry so you can blow us all up."

"I'm not actually a terrorist scoping out the ferry so I can
blow us all up."

"If you are, at least do me the favour of doing it when I'm
not working."

"If I am and if you'd prefer, I'll at least do you the favour of
doing it when you're not working."

"Better yet, tell me where it's going to be so I can be on a part
of the ship where I'll survive and get a nice insurance payout or at
least a bunch of paid time off to deal with the PTSD and shit."

"Sure."

He's staring at his feet. I'm losing him. "So, really then.
What's that all about? What's the deal?"

"I would have thought it was self-explanatory."

"Why don't you help a dullard out a little."

"Don't you have to be living in the most opaque of bubbles
to not be brimming with hate over what's going on, all the
time?"

"Well, my bubble could probably do with a cleaning, but..."

He takes a sip of his drink. "Maybe you're too selfish to hate like you should."

Like I said, *Fucker* or what? "Fuck you old man. It's you *men* who have fucked up this world. Particularly you *old* men. Don't go taking it out on fucking me."

"Yeah, I guess..."

"Is this all just Vietnam stuff?"

"Vietnam *stuff*," he says, his tone never more reflective of our age difference. "What's Vietnam but Germany and Uganda and Syria and Palestine and the back seat of cop cars and solitary confinement and darkened bedrooms and what goes on behind locked doors the world over?"

"So you lost your kid? What happened? Actually terrorists? *What?*"

He doesn't answer, won't or can't, but the pallor that comes over his face tries to.

"You said you write this to get rid of it. All your writing's like that? Is that what you're doing while you sit there rumming yourself up and running your pencil down?"

"Pretty much."

"Fucking hell."

"Anyway, what about you? Tell me about your app that's going to make you your *gajillions*. I need to get in on that. A fraction of a gajillion'll probably go all the way I need it to."

"I can't... It's too, *embryonic*. But it's an app that will basically make everyone happy. It'll make them believe in themselves, do what they want to do. Like the wealthiest people with their teams of yes-men. How they sleep at night. Based on the flexibility of truth. You know, difference between guilt and innocence is the quality of your lawyer, and, well all that. And it's going to get bought up for a jaw-dropping lot of money. Those San Fran tech guys, they have literally billions to throw at things. You know how much Google's worth? And don't dare say it. Fucking please. I know. Fat and flat. Fat and flat. You want to hear the song some grade nine girls made up about it? Good.

But I know, it's what I am, and it's the opposite of what you need to be to get anywhere in this male-dumbinated world. I'm not stupid. I'm fat and flat and as good an idea as I might have, I risk killing it by being ugly. So I'm already starting to work out, running, up to twenty minutes now. And I've totally stopped on chocolate, and… and I'll buy what I need to buy, ultimately. You know?"

"But…"

"Yeah, sure. *But.* You couldn't get hard and I wouldn't either. I know, Alex's dad, what got him up? Believe me, I know what you're thinking, this is the schmuck that's my boy's dad, his genetic inheritance? Sometimes when I used to look at Alex I'd see his dad and I'd think… *fuck*, what I'd *think*! But I have to have faith that genetics only mean so much, and there are lots of successful people out there that have right cunts for parents, right? A lot of them. I'll be another one of them. Happiness is beneficial for the body, but it's grief that develops the mind."

"The saddest thing I've ever heard."

"But accurate. Do you know what it's like to look at your child and see traces of an ass? Do you? If you do, then I feel as sorry for you as I feel for myself. One's child should be half who you love, and half yourself… who hopefully you also love, right?"

"…I don't know. I wonder if love really does us any favours. Evolutionarily speaking, it certainly serves its purpose, but for individual existences? I think it's possible to love too much."

Well, tell me because I want to know—what if I did love Alex even more than I do? Would I be incapacitated? And of course that leaves me feeling like a complete piece of shit waste of breath excuse for a mother if I don't love my child as much as the next mother. As much as princess Kate. Which makes me wonder if that's because my boy's just less loveable than hers. And that makes me think HOLY FUCK, brain, just shut the fuck up for once just once fuck please!

He's sitting there on my who-knows-just-how-used sofa with his drink in his tight hands, holding on, like a man in a storm in an ocean clinging onto a buoy placed there by god himself just to save him. No, it's more like when I was watching him the first time on top deck, like he's in a crowd of people pressing against him, the drink a pole he's holding onto to not be carried away. Why this sense of him being pulled away? It's just me? My own fear of losing a rare buoy? Which is pretty problematical.

"I guess life certainly was simpler before I had Alex. But now I've got a purpose. Someone to work for."

"But he's adopted now."

"*No.* Just permanent custody. I get to see him three times a year and he'll always know me, and most importantly, my lawyer said I have the right to bring back my case to court any time I think I can convince a judge to give custody back to me. And that's going to happen in two or three years. Again, once I sell Paul and, well, I already told you."

"How far along are you with this Paul?"

"Some days it feels like it's just over there, others…"

9.

NEXT DAY HE caught the morning ferry to Sydney and I slept all day and worked all the next night on Paul and then worked a non-return to Sydney and spent the night there. And fine, because you're asking, I'll tell you that I stayed in the Thompson hotel, a rooming house that I use when I don't have the return to work. We get a stipend when we have to stay on the non-home end, which is enough to at least get a Day's Inn, but I go for the cheapest place and pocket the rest. The sooner I can get the breast implants, the better. In summer I'd sleep in a park if it was safe, but even for the still fat and flat amongst us, that's just tempting fate. When a man wants to harm a woman, the size of her thighs hardly matters. Well, I hope anyway.

And here I am working the shift back to PAB and there he is, in what's become his usual spot, the table by the forward-facing window two to starboard right in front of the window. If it were summer he'd have to sacrifice some dignity in madly rushing for it, like people rushing the door at the opening of a walk-in clinic, or Black Friday's onslaught of rabid idiots. But he wouldn't, he's not the type, he'd sit in a windowless corner with a cold draft before doing such a thing. That's something I guess that draws me to him.

I ask what I can get him and of course he gives me that half-look, which I can't decide if it's shyness, disconnect, or dear prudence, and says just a can of Pepsi please. And a glass. And the more the afternoon wears on and I think about it, the more it pisses me off. I mean, be honest, right? In the top ten list of moral instruction, from fortune cookie to Torah, right? But none of us are. I'm not, and don't you claim to be either. There is not a one amongst us. Why's it so hard? I don't know.

Right. Bullshit. I'm lying right now. Glass houses again. Which is not to suggest that my mom's fucking wise, because good lord how she isn't—she's just looking for others to drag down to her level in the hopes that a just god wants to be loved and when it's pointed out to him that we're all jerks he's not about to kill us all because who'll be left to lick his feet. Fine. I guess she's a bit wise. We all have our moments. Stopped clocks. But they're only right those two times because of the limited superficial information they give. And you delve down into microseconds and all that and they're right so rarely it'd probably be a challenge to find a thing that's reliably less truthful.

Paul might say *Give me six lines written by the hand of an honest man, and I'll find something in them which will hang him.* No one wants to hang and we're all a bunch of actors who'd rather you catch us in our biggest lie than uncover our deepest truths.

But tell you something you don't know, right?

"It's my lunch break. Wanna think about coming with?"

"Sure," he says, a co-worker who didn't realise he gets breaks and isn't sure he needs one.

I tell him I want to go to the top deck and so he puts on his winter coat—which is an expensive looking late model North Face Everest-peaking thingy that I can imagine he put a bunch of money into not so much to ensure he'd be dry and warm, but to make sure he was sure that he was indeed serious about what he was doing. My own coat's a cobbled together net of rags in comparison, but he doesn't offer me his, and I realise with clarity no one has ever offered me their coat in my life. Feels like that should make me feel sadder than it does, and somehow that makes me happy, boosts my confidence in how different I can expect my future to be.

The wind is blustery and there's no real respite from it, so to make something of it, to add more contrast to how much better my future life is going to be, I lead us out to the middle of the helipad and sit down in the lap of the bottom of the H, facing forward. James sits down across from me, perfectly placed inside the white lines and facing aft.

"You got anything to eat?"

"Peebeenjay" he says, "But I don't eat it until 5:00."

"I never see you eating. Not even snacking."

"I try to focus. But it's also… most animals go long periods of not eating. And our food has so many toxins. Moral baggage, too, of course. Number one rule of sailing. Keep the ocean out of the boat."

"That'd be why you're so skinny, then?"

He says nothing and I pull my fake meat, cucumber and sriracha sandwich out of my pocket and take a bite. It tastes different out here in the cold. More like the cold, hardly-hearty, unloving, unsatisfying, so-called sustenance that it barely is.

For something to say I tell him more about my English teacher in high school, how he was a bit of a celebrity, and the entirety of the teaching staff resented him and probably half of them worried that he was molesting the hottest amongst us (so don't worry about me!). His celebrity was from having a couple of novels published, not best-sellers or anything, but still, you could get them on Amazon. And the town library had some copies, so of course we all read the sex and violence parts. Probably would have been fired if the teacher's union wasn't so strong. Plus he was blatantly gay. His sex scenes were straight, though. Guess he wasn't that brave. Maybe he was just smart.

"On the first day of class he talked about intelligence suffering from the division of science and the arts, and how they were never meant to be so separate. He assigned us an essay to read and I actually read all twenty-eight pages of it." This never came up in our science class, and I asked about that once and he said he'd asked the science teacher if he wanted to do some joint curriculum, but that Mr. Sandstone had thought he was propositioning him. And then he laughed, but I'm not sure he was joking. "I told him the one problem with the essay was that it seemed to say science and scientists are *more* important that art and artists. He looked at me hard, and then he nodded his head and smiled. I felt so understood, so deep. It made me feel so smart. In that moment I had such high hopes for myself, wanted to feel that over and over and over again."

"So what happened?" says James, and it's a fine fucking question, isn't it?

"Teenage depression, I guess, awareness of the shit state of the world, body dysmorphia in a world run by men lusting for power and violence. Drugs... Reality, basically."

He looks at me with such sad eyes that I have to look away.

"I had a teacher in high school," he tries, "who told us she would give a bonus five percent on our final grade to anyone who read Don Quixote over the term."

"Did you do it?"

"No. No one did. It's a thousand pages."

Thinking of Mr. Graham and science and art and the way he made me feel, and my geezer here, makes me think of PTP in a way that is almost desperate. Worried, I guess, but I can't think of why exactly. Nothing to do with not getting it done or it not selling, just...

"You ever hear of wave readers?" he says now, looking out at the strangely calm sea. It's as if all the blustery cross currents of winds are cancelling each other out. But surely we're leaving a wake?

"Nope."

"There are people, aboriginal island dwellers, that can go out on a boat on the ocean with no compass, and they can read the swells and wave patterns and sense land out there. They think this is how ancient people spread to far flung islands. Imagine the in-tuneness-with-the-universe, to be able to do such a thing?"

"The opposite of your number one rule of sailing."

He looks at me. "I guess that's true eh? They become the ocean, take it all inside them."

That is pretty wild.

"I wonder what we're doing to such senses with all our cell phones and staring into them all the time, using GPS to direct us where we're going without even bothering to pay attention to a single marker on the way there. What's that doing to our sense of self in a place?"

"What's all that doing to our sense of self in general?" I hear myself say, and it's another damn good question. The artful scientist is not the one who gives the right answers, but the one who asks the questions, so a big fucking hooray for me.

There's silence a while as I finish my sandwich and feel the gigantic chugging of the engine at the heart of this massive heap of steel ploughing its ungainly way through the water. Will it last the whole way?

"Now that I think about it, I guess over the last few months I've been feeling that more. Getting outside of myself but also letting the inside in. Like I'm being dissolved, but still aware. I think it's a good thing."

"Probably just death coming."

"…It makes me want to seize some kind of control over things. Steer the ship."

"Makes sense."

"Like when we'd descend into a hot landing zone. Sitting helpless on our helmets, hoping it will catch the bullet intent on tearing into us unceremoniously through our asses. You sit and you sit and you pray the searing hot steel doesn't come and you're desperate to land and get into the thick of it so at least you can shoot at something, have the slightest semblance of control and effect, rather than just sitting there, shamefully dependent on luck, nothing but luck. Bullet in the eye instead of the ass at least."

"We're all just sitting on our helmets, hoping."

"Those Vendée sailors, they don't have the comfort of ready rescue. They're so isolated it can take days for a ship to reach them, and by then… There was one in '97, Jerry Roufs, disappeared. Dead. Into the great whereafter. The waves out there, they call them mountains they're so tall. Up to eight storeys trough to crest. Just imagine yourself in the middle of that, you and your little boat. And rogue waves out of nowhere. No one to save you. And never mind the waves, every moment wondering am I about to hit a shipping container?"

"You have to be mostly crazy," I tell him. Thinking about the emptiness and the cold, I hug myself tighter and look up, wanting to see a bird or something, but there's none out here. "You ever heard of *the singularity*?" I ask him.

"Not really."

So I explain it to him best I can and he looks at me, looks at the sea, looks at the ground, sits cross-legged the whole time and I think about how the geezer's knees should be hurting by now. But I guess those old buddhas sit for hours meditating just fine. Maybe he's one of them. It's annoying me how he's not looking more surprised at what I'm telling him. "Well?" I say.

"Pauline, it's just… this faith we have in microchips. Solving everything. And now, we'll download ourselves into them? Become them? Even if you think humanity's got significance without a soul, it's…"

I tell him you never know, because really you don't.

"If we become able to live for centuries or more, who's going to be able to afford to do it? Billions will just keep dying at younger and younger ages as the climate goes to hell. Ferraris are nice cars, but I don't get too excited about them because I'm never going to have one and it just makes them ugly knowing that the only people that can own them are people who can stomach that the money they spent on the car they're driving could give a bunch of kids food in the belly and a good education and hope."

"Yeah… hope that they can grow up and be successful and buy Ferraris," I say, mostly to annoy him, but also because it feels like it should be said. "And technology keeps getting cheaper for everybody. What percentage of the world's population had a fridge or even a lamp fifty years ago?"

"And that's not even factoring in what most of them did to get that money in the first place," he carries on, ignoring me. "The whole system's skewed and corrupt and there's barely a shred of it I can condone."

Geezer's got issues, but don't we all. "Well, I don't see any-one offering a better system. And we are who we are. And you can only help so many. And you better help yourself and your kind first, especially if the future is going to be so bad as you say. And defeating *death?* Even if only a few can do it, that's, like, the greatest human achievement. The one thing we were supposedly never going to be able to do."

"You're probably right. Taxes were also supposedly something we'd never beat yet plenty do."

"There you go! That's the spirit!" I say and give him a shove, but he barely smiles. My, those lips of his are stiff. Almost as stiff as I'm getting in this cold. "And with my Paul, I'm going to have a good shot at being someone who can live forever. Me and Alex. Maybe I'll spring for you, too," I try.

"Living forever is the last thing I'm signing up for," he says, without a laugh or a thank you for my generosity. "There are people I want to be with on the other side. There's no one here that I fancy spending an eternity with."

"No offense taken," I say and laugh. But you know what, fuck you old holier than thou geezer. "Not even if you had the dick of a fifteen-year-old?" I try, but get no rise out of him (☺).

I'm done my sandwich, which eases my soul no more than this conversation and I wish I had something sweet to follow, but this is me limiting my sugar intake to the properly recommended four teaspoons per day. As of yesterday. Which is going to be hard, considering even *bread* has sugar in it.

"My wife," he suddenly says, and fuck do I brace myself. This conversation has been all over the place, but talk about rogue waves! "She died at thirty-four. We had a vacation planned, back to Spain, my boy had never been. He was three. Two weeks before we're due to leave she wakes up with a swollen stomach. We bring her to hospital and next day they tell me to sit down. Tell me it looks like cancer. Tell me she may not have long left to live. I bit my fist, so hard. I almost froze, seized up. There was no way. But there was a way. Of course there was a damn way. Lots of them. We went for chemo. Five days later, the third session, the oncologist tells me there's no point, in a week she'll be dead no matter what we do to her."

I want to call him on this. No way they could know it was going to happen that fast. Guess it's important he tell it this way. Or maybe in his olden days, in the old country, this is how shit went down.

"He tried to make me have her stay at the hospital and I told him I was bringing her home, since it made no difference anyway. I put her on the sofa. Couldn't put her in bed, not in the middle of the day. Admitting too much. I tried to comfort her. We told each other it would pass, a miracle was going to happen, she would be fine. Because what else do you say to each other? The second night, I lay by her side, I held her wrist, feeling her pulse, feeling her alive, but now believing, it seemed almost impossible that that weak throbbing could continue, so delicate and miraculous. And at eighteen minutes before five in the morning, I will never forget that time, it stopped. Every river in the world stopped flowing, except for the current of rage and anger within me. I took her clothes off, I bathed her, I dressed her in her favourite dress, and then I..."

His voice sounds younger, stronger, yet distant, as though it's the old him, the young him, the him of her, speaking through this current him, the years that have grown around him like tree rings, strangling him. He's holding that wrist still. Actually, he's holding his own wrist, in his lap, his legs still crossed. Head down and I can't tell if his eyes are open. And my damn eyes are stinging, but still no tears from the stone that is me.

"Wait a second!" I say, realising it suddenly, and grabbing his wrist with his broken watch on it. "Seriously? All these years you've worn this like this?"

He looks at me with clear eyes. Guess he's all cried out. "I was holding her, dead, and all I could hear was the ticking of this watch, pounding on the absence. I threw it against the wall. A few other things too. Later I was going to throw it away, but then it seemed like the one thing that would keep her alive in me somehow."

He pulls his arm back into himself and speaks to his lap. "I have her buried in a graveyard under a monument taller than me. A picture of her I have to replace every year because the sun fades it. My name's on the thing too... my year of birth, and a dash. I used to hate seeing that on tombstones, just hate it, because I only thought of the living still. When she died I wanted that on there. I wanted her to know that I was coming too. To wait because I'd be with her before long. That I had no intention of doing anything other than joining her. But now... What if I died now and found this me in heaven encountering that her of decades ago; we'd be so different. How would we relate? I'm not the me she knew."

"Time only exists because we're here to measure it. Outside of that measuring, it all exists at once, or, basically not at all. If your wife is dead and gone, so is her time. She got to fast forward to the end, step outside of time. To her, you've already joined her. You're already dead."

"Is that supposed to be comforting?"

"Well, I'm not selling a religion here, but..."

I GOT MY first real app assignment completed! It's a far cry from a functioning Pep-Talk Paul, being as it is just essentially a fancily presented quote search engine, but it runs smoothly and does what it's supposed to do. And there's something to be said for fancy. And when I use it some of the quotes I get in return do make me feel more reassured so there's proof of my Paul concept right there!

But it did hit me, that PTP differs from literature in that books suggest answers to questions they themselves pose, or at least they lead you along a path of wonder that fills your head with questions you want answers to, and that's the beauty, the inspiration of it, Kafka's axe for the frozen sea within us. But with PTP, *you* pose the questions. Do you know what questions to ask? That's the point of art, answers are not the hard part, it's having the depth and creativity to think of meaningful, novel questions. I guess this is the limit of PTP's ability to make the world ultimately a better place. But fuck, I can only do so much, and happiness is personal anyway. If I'm happy in my head what does it matter to me what those fuckers over there are doing in their own heads? PTP's offering to make you happy, not necessarily deep or caring or anything. Whatever. Like someone buys antibiotics for an infection—they're not looking to make the whole damn lot of us better off, just their own body. Do we always have to find something so wrong in someone doing something purely for themselves now and fucking then?

I didn't get the return trip on my out to Sydney so I stayed the night and hung out in Sydney for the day and did some Christmas shopping for Alex. Even bought James something. I'll tell you what when I give it to him. Now here I am working back to PAB and James is aboard and I feel, what, *happy*? He updated me on the Vendée, stuff I already know because I've been following it myself and it might have even given me an idea for my next assignment. At this point I'm pretending I know nothing of what he tells me because I think he likes having someone to tell who seems at least a little impressed by it. He's writing away and drinking his Pepsi and rum and I should probably tell him he needs to cut down on his sugar. Start taking his booze straight like a real man. Guy's gonna die of sugar poisoning. No way for a sailor to go. Surely a real sailor needs a salty death!

I come up behind him and he's scribbling away, a captain filling his log before going down with his ship. Believing in people caring. I consider trying to read it, but can't invade his privacy like that. Plus, do I really want more evidence that this guy I'm about to do a little road trip with could end up hacking me to pieces in a rage?

"Last call, James," I say and he tells me he's fine. Smiles as though he barely knows me, and goes back to his writing. What the fuck? Did I do something wrong? I think twice about inviting him, but I've already gone over it and over it and decided we need to do this and so to hell with him. "James, I want to take a little road trip with you," I say.

He takes off his glasses, folds his notebook closed and places them upon it. He looks at me more directly, somehow, than he yet has. Or maybe I'm just always too scattered to notice how intense his look is. "A road trip?" he says.

"Yes. Almost exactly seven hundred kilometres according to Google maps. Bit of a ways, especially in this season. But you need to see the place and I need to see it again. Haven't been since a grade-five school trip."

No lights light him up. "Where to?" he says simply, and his tone is that of an employee asking for clarification of what he knows he has to do, and I like that.

"L'Anse Aux Meadows. You must know it."

"Of course. All us Spaniards know it," he says with a wink and a smile, which I'll take as positive.

"You ever been?"

"No."

"You want to have?"

"Have what?"

"*Been.* Do you want to have been? Do you wanna *go*?"

"That's the far north tip, right?"

"Yep. We'll rent a car and go right from the terminal. Make it there for sunrise."

"What's the hurry?"

"You need some land miles under you. See more of the Rock than lousy old PAB."

I have to do a round so I pass amongst my twelve tables, share pleasantries and gather glasses and no one wants any more drinks because they're all sensible enough to know they're going to be driving off this boat in an hour and best do so seeing only one road to follow.

Only one road to follow. That has to be me. From now on. I have to fucking focus. I run another load of glasses, thinking about just how far off Paul I actually am, and it depresses me like nothing ever. This little trip will be about motivation, about focusing on what's important and what's not. There really only is one thing.

The winds and currents were friendly on the crossing, so it was only six and a half hours, about as fast as you can hope for, and we docked just past six. We got in my car, discussed renting something more reliable than a twelve-year-old Toyota and James, with his knowledge of cars from thirty-five years behind the wheel of a Toronto taxi, said there isn't anything, really, but since we're going so remote, he felt it best we rent an SUV. He was willing to pay half so we rented a RAV4 and I can't remember the last time I was in a brand-new car. After stopping in at my place to get warm clothes for me and a bunch of blankets and pillows and thermal underwear, just in case, and then hitting the superstore for food and the NLC for rum, it's after nine by the time we're putting Corner Brook behind us and are through Deer Lake (where we filled up and also bought a jerry-can of gas—it is winter and there isn't much along this highway) and on the 430, the highway that will take us all the way there. The dark we drive through is cold, with an air of fuck-off-and-leave-me-alone about it.

I'm tired, but excited to be getting out and doing something! If there be a better reason why people should pair up, go ahead and tell me 'cause it'd be good to know. He's sleeping right now because I told him he needs to sleep off his booze so he can drive later.

It's one in the morning and we've just passed Port Saunders and it's two-hundred and twenty kilometres to LAM and I can barely keep my eyes open and I need to stop or pass on to James. Deciding it probably best to let James get a proper sleep and drive the rest of the way in daylight, I pull over to sleep.

He's got his seat reclined all the way so I can't sleep in the back, but the driver's seat reclines almost flat so it's fine. I throw a blanket over him and get myself set up and get comfy and feel warm enough but wonder how cold it's going to get but assume one of us will wake up before we freeze to death and if we don't, then what the hell, we've achieved the dream of dying in our sleep; and it's only minus twelve anyway, so let's not all get all carried away with ourselves. My mind again is wondering what the fuck I'm doing here and with this geezer of all guys and geezers, but seeing's how I've been working all day I'm pretty tired and fall asleep before my mind's even made up its mind as to whether or not I should have myself a slug of rum.

11.

I WAKE UP on the verge of shivering and don't for a second not know exactly where I am. I gather the blankets in close but they make me no warmer. James is awake, just sitting there, staring out the window like some dumb cat warm on a sunny sill.

"Holy fuck, James," I say. "It's fucking freezing! You could have turned the fucking car on," I say, as I sit up and do it myself.

"Good morning sunshine," he says.

By the time I've stepped out and pissed in the ditch I'm colder yet, and there's still no warm air coming through.

"Sleep okay?" he asks.

The sun's above the horizon and has not a single cloud for company. "What time is it?"

"8:04."

I get the bag of food and take out a bottle of coffee, then hand the bag to him.

He takes out a sandwich and rips the wrapper off in the manner of one used to eating this way. Guess he's probably also used to sitting in a freezing car.

"I woke up last night to go to the washroom and you wouldn't believe it," he says. "I've never seen stars like that. Never. In the desert, probably, but I was looking at them with very different eyes."

"I'm glad you liked them," I say, feeling my usual morning fog of grumpy, made infinitely worse by waking up cold.

"Not sure *liked* is the word, actually. It felt like I was being fragmented, pulled apart and sucked up into it all. Consumed, you know?"

Finally some warmth coming out of the vents. "Well, that's basically what you told me you wanted for yourself now. Remember? Instead of being buried?"

"I've never felt such a sense of distance, like I'm here and everything else is way out there, a whole lot of nothing in between. I've never felt farther from an answer. Or the people I've loved."

"I saw something the other day about some physicist who's working at a scale so small that it's comparable to how small a speck of dust is to the overall size of our universe."

"So that universe out there is mirrored by the same distances inside us?"

"The same emptiness, too. If an atom were the size of the earth, the proton would be only 200 meters in diameter with its electrons spinning around the equator. Talk about a whole hell of a lot of nothing."

"How does one even begin to wrap their head around that? I mean…"

"We don't. I don't think even they do. It's just theoretical."

"You might have a point there."

"As long as you say so."

"Well, might as well get going, eh?" he says and I agree, hoping the passing scenery, which is supposedly some of the most beautiful in the world, will keep his thoughts occupied. In a few minutes' time we're passing right along the ocean's edge and with the low sun and clear blue sky and glittering calm ocean the beauty is overwhelming. It brings me down somehow.

"I've been thinking a lot about your singularity business," he says now, and I kind of want to tell him to stop talking, but I did invite him on this trip and so I should probably at least limit my bitch commands. "Imagine if you knew you were going to live forever, but only as long as you don't *accidentally* die. Would probably pull the rug out from under the whole extreme sport business, eh? Probably even travel. Leaving the house at all. We'd never have another Vendée, I'm sure. Everyone would become afraid of really *living* life. Imagine what you'd be risking? Fear of death would go through the roof. Get hit by a bus and you miss out on eternity."

"Probably, eh?"

"But it might solve terrorism. Not just because of what it would do to the idea of suicide and life after death, but what it would do to history. Terrorist ideals are rooted in a longing for an idealized past. So many people want to get back to the good old days of tradition and constancy, simplicity, knowability. Religion and political dogmatism and idealism leads people to these mythical beliefs that are wholly unfounded, but allow you to feel part of something bigger than yourself, something important and worthwhile, something you need to fight for, something that will survive you after you die, and you'll go on in that. But if there were real immortality, well, it would change all that, not to mention how it would force you to re-examine your relationship to science and fact in general. And imagine dying for the ones you love, expecting to meet them in the afterlife, but they live on forever in this world?"

"I guess."

"...You guess? That's it?"

"I guess."

"Come on, Pauline. *Try.* You're smarter than you want to admit."

"Pardon fucking me?" I say, wondering if he needs a good punch in the face, but I don't because he's fucking driving. "Conceit really doesn't suit you."

"I'm sorry. I *guess.*"

"I *guess* what you're using too many words as usual to explain is that if people become able to live forever, the lie will be put to life after death, and everyone will start trying to make the most of their one life and look forward instead of backward."

"Basically, yes."

"Well duh, not exactly ground-breaking ideas here. You going to wow me next by telling me science casts light?"

"Ideas don't have to be ground-breaking to be profound. In need of restating," he answers, his delivery guarded, humbled. That's better.

"We better also remember here then that a lot of people who kill just do so out of anger and revenge. Profit too of course. And lots are just jerk-bags doing it to feel big and important. Manly."

"My main point is that I *guess* you're helping me realise we really need to start looking more to the future and embracing that, instead of glorifying a past that wasn't at all what we think it was. And I include myself in that. And I've even started writing—"

"Well don't get too excited. All the tech gods out there, the billionaires I'm going to join soon enough, they talk about a future where everything will be better and perfect, but does it ever really look like arriving? *The end justifies the means, but what if the end never comes?* There are some scary sad-ass problems that are far from easily solved and will likely result in billions dying before too long at all, and having a smart thermostat on the market that costs more than the majority of people on the planet could afford on a month's wages, never even mind owning the home that it would smartly monitor the temperature of, is not exactly cause for hope or cause to smugly walk around prouder than Jesus H after he turned water to wine." Well holy shit, look at me go.

"And here I thought I was agreeing with you," he says. He looks like he has a lot more to add, like an actor on stage fighting to hold back his laughter, to stay in character, remember a line, but he falls silent. And that's fine with me.

We pass the town of St. Lunaire, which has an Esso—and a café called Dark Tickle!—but we're still at a quarter tank and LAM's only fifteen clicks, so we press on along the decent road through a rolling landscape of snow-covered brush and short trees, passing a Parks Canada sign in its traditional forest green and white announcing L'Anse Aux Meadows and we carry on another minute and come to a left turnoff, with another Parks Canada sign.

"Sign says closed," he says, no disappointment in his voice at all.

"Well, just keep going… Look, that sign. Says there's a village and restaurant up there."

Another few hundred meters up the road we come to a T-Junction. Directly ahead is a snow-covered, big-rock-strewn bay.

To our right is the direction to go for a restaurant and an art gallery, while left, as far as the sign's concerned, has nothing, though that's the direction of the LAM sight. I tell James to go left and he does and a couple minutes later we've reached the end of the road. The GPS shows we're at the very tip of the peninsula, as far north as you can drive on this island. Top of The Rock. It also tells us that we're only about a ten-minute walk from the actual LAM sight, though it does not tell us whether there are fences or dogs or spike-bottomed-pits ensuring that closed means closed when it comes to Parks Canada. A light snow's falling, yet the sun's making the most of its opportunities between the clouds as they roll expeditiously by.

"You want to try and see it?" I say.

After a while he says, "No. Not right now, anyway."

"Okay, what next then?"

He doesn't answer. He's staring out the windshield at the cold, white-capping waters beyond the snow and ice. I guess seeing the buildings, the attempts at establishing a place to call home, is not nearly as impressive as looking out at these rocks and this sea, unchanged in a thousand years, that those original Vikings would have navigated and got their feet wet and cold wading through to step on land for the first time in god knows how long, hard earth that they couldn't have known their feet or their hands or their asses would ever feel again when setting off from the other side of the Atlantic. Did they know there was something else out there? With Columbus we know what he didn't know, but with these Vikings, we don't. But they must have known that they didn't really know shit, and so heading off on trips such as that one, well, they probably pretty much knew they were ultimately fucked, like the ships that are supposedly within a decade going to carry their hardy-but-hapless human crew to Mars. Then again, maybe others had visited before them and come back to tell the story. Or most likely, duh, they set off with excited certainty because their gods had come to them in dreams or drunken trances and given them guidance and so they set off with more confidence than Columbus or any of us wanna-be Mars colonizers will ever manage to muster.

Gods. So easy to forget about them.

"Imagine what it was like to sail in those days," James says.

"That's what I'm—"

"The scurvy. The bleeding from the gums and the madness. The way you'd be coolly stabbed or strangled by your shipmates at first sign of it, because they know there's no cure and it's only going to get worse and so unquestionably best for everyone to just take you out early. Nothing personal."

"Guess that's another reason, beyond not having to wipe the toilet seat, that it's better to sail alone."

He looks at me and smiles. "You make me laugh, you know?" he says, not actually laughing, of course. In fact, I realise I'm not sure I've ever witnessed him doing such a thing. And I realise I really don't want to.

We go to Norseman's Village Restaurant and B&B and it's closed, but back down the highway a bit at the village we find a takeout called St. Snows, and there we order fish and chips because that's what they say they do well, but they clearly don't care to watch their customers enjoy their food, as they offer no seating. So we're back in the car and staring at the rocky coastline that I hope to James is interesting but I'm sorry to say really feels no different than any other Newfoundland coast of the kind I've stared at all my life. Maybe it's just that I'm not a god-is-in-the-details kind of person, but you have to be careful with such people, because most of them are just plain and painfully anal. The fish and chips are good. Just the right crispiness, and nice thick fillets.

Just to remind him that he's not alone, I say, "Imagine this is a far sight better than what those stinky old Norseman subsisted on."

"Can't imagine they had ketchup," he says, eying my empty packets on the dash.

We finish in silence and I'm really tired now. "Let's go find that hotel. St Brennan's?"

"St Brendan's."

He puts the car in drive, but doesn't move. I sense he's about to really open up to me, but he lets his foot off the brake and we move ostensibly forward.

12.

IT'S A THOROUGHLY unfrilly affair, but there's space for us, and with minimal fuss and few words we make the arrangements at the front desk attended to by an old First Nations woman who would clearly rather be sleeping but still manages to smile and throw in a dear or two, and we go to our room. Is there anything better than being called 'my dear' by someone who can pull it off? I step into our room and he follows me, and it's nice and tidy and even clean-smelling in a way that isn't all about chemicals. The curtains are closed and when I throw them open it's a yard and playground area. I close the curtains again.

James inspects the place, then sits down on the bed furthest from the window.

"You must need a drink," I say to him.

"It can't hurt," he says.

"I think that's called kicking the can down the road."

"At my age that's the name of the game," he says.

"Solid progress, eh?"

I hand him the bottle and he takes it from me like it's all he needs and wants, then takes a long pull. He doesn't even cringe. Which is slightly worrying.

"You know…" he says, leaving it out there, and I tell him I don't. His face looks pained somewhat, like he wants to tell me something he wishes I already knew. Which makes me wonder about living in a world where we know all the stories there are to be told.

"I had some customers who were native," he says, and I brace myself. "I hate to say it, but most of them were drunk or high or something you don't want to be when you're talking to the cops or meeting a girl's mother."

He says this in a way that is asking for no comments, like an actor on stage delivering a line and expecting nothing unexpected. At his age he should know better, but I indulge him and remain silent. But he doesn't continue, so I say, "Aren't most of the people you drive at night drunk?"

"This one night, this guy flags me down and I stop and he's half-in and then there's these two guys pulling at him. *No fucking way you squaw's* what I hear. *You fucking dirty bogan's* what I hear next. And he's so sloppily drunk, all he's got left is grunts, not even token resistance, gave up on the fight long ago. So I get out of my cab and it's two white guys, letting go of the drunk now and standing up to lowly old cab-driver me, and they tell me the *Indian's* got no money that's his own anyway, and don't get involved with shit that obviously doesn't concern raghead cabbies from Iraq or some other sandy shithole."

He takes another hit of the rum. He's right back there.

"I stepped right up to the one with the beard, and I said to him, 'He's my customer now, and if you lay one more hand on him, I'll unlay it, and then I'm calling the police.' He blinked. Like they always do, even despite the liquid courage. 'And while we wait for them,' I said, 'I'll gladly rip your wanna-be white-boy terrorist beard off and crush your skull and mush your bullshit little brains to pulp under my boots. Because maybe I've been waiting for just this moment.' You know, just trying to make them think I am some terrorist who might actually do that stuff."

"It felt good."

"It felt even better when the guy took a swing at me."

"So much for respecting your elders."

"I managed to duck it, and he fell over with the force he'd put into it, and I bent over and grabbed him by his ridiculous beard, not that I have anything against beards, I guess, but I had something against his, and I kneed him in the jaw, and then I punched him in it, and I felt a breakage, like two Lego pieces coming undone. 'I'm a taxpayer too,' I told them. And then—"

"You did fucking not. You actually said that?"

"And then the cops were there, and I got charged with assault, and convicted, and got probation and anger management and a suspended sentence, but, well."

"Wow. Good for you, I guess. And I'm sure it would have been different if it was a white guy you'd been defending against two native drunks."

"You think?" he says, managing to keep a straight face. "I do feel bad for them."

"Who?"

"...All of them, I suppose. The racist cops and the lawyers and judges, but I was thinking of the two guys. I know they don't want that, of course, but..." He takes another swig, and it's not just that he's drinking straight, there seems to be something needy about the way he does it, like an addict using it to punch away pain.

"Yeah, but, well, natives. Somehow they need to start getting their act together."

"Easy for white people, *you*, to say."

Ooo, there's some acid in there? Interesting. He better be careful.

"Try being not white, see how easy it is in this racist world. You know how many people look at me lately like I might be about to whip out a machine gun and mow them all down?"

"But you kind of *are*."

"Why do you think I go to the trouble of shaving this hair on my face every day? Beards are all well and good if your skin colour shows you're not a terrorist, but if it doesn't, every white person looks at you like you're the commander of ISIS."

"Or a vain, wanna-be-manly, paint-by-numbers doofus," I try. "Why *do* you look so... I mean, you're Spanish."

"There's always been a large Muslim presence and influence in Spain, from the Umayyad over a thousand years ago to the Moroccan's who came to fight in the civil war. Especially Southwest Spain, which is where I'm originally from. Ever heard of the Alhambra?"

"Oh."

"The worst thing is that your hate for those sadists is more extreme than anyone's. If one of them was standing in front of you right now you would tear his head off." With that he takes another swig of the rum, and turns away and fishes his notebook and pencil out of his bag and tells me he needs to do some writing.

Who am I, so I flick on the TV and there's sports or politics or cooking on basically every channel and I leave it on a cupcake-making competition with mother and daughter teams battling it out for ten grand that they seem so desperate to win you'd think they must be living in proper poverty and never learned math in school and have no idea that ten thousand dollars isn't going to do shit to change anything for them in the long run. I pour some rum into a glass for myself and take a sip and tell me how people drink this stuff straight? I look at James and he's scribbling away into his notebook with all the inflamed intensity you might imagine of Tolstoy or whoever. And it freaks me out thinking about him writing that shit with me right here in this shit little room with him. Or maybe he's finally gotten it out and he's writing about love peace and harmony now?

The judges are now discussing how the one team's cupcakes, in the shape of aliens, was really true to the visual theme of aliens, but the other team used the sweet potato flavour theme more effectively and they're ready to name the winner and so they call in both mother-daughter pairs and announce the winners, and said winners jump around like idiots and the losing pair hug one another and try to look happy for the other team but it's plain to see that if they could they'd stab them through the heart and take their money. Okay, I'm exaggerating—the mother has that look, the kid is trying to smile but looking like she wants to run away and never compete in another competition so long as she lives because she realises she'll never win anything ever again and what the fuck is she even doing here (Okay, yes, still exaggerating a little, but what of it? And it's not untrue, only bent truth.)

Why do I watch this shit? I turn the TV off, but then it seems too dark and dead and so I turn it back on, stick it on a soccer game and turn the volume down, then pull out my computer and my Bose speaker and I put my coding playlist on. I look to James and the level of the rum in his bottle indicates he's clearly intent on drinking faster than his body can metabolize. And he's still wrangling with his pencil, totally Tolstoying it. Now he stops to sharpen his pencil, and he does this with a cool calm grace that's scary. Like if you saw that in your executioner you would know it was game over, no hope in hell or anywhere else for mercy.

I take another sip myself and take a look at the Vendée page and see that Armel has widened his lead over Alex. Come on Alex! Don't let that broken foil get you down!

I close out of all my browsers, turn the wi-fi off to help me focus, and get down to work on my coding. And soon I'm getting into it, the alcohol freeing me up while also narrowing my focus to the task at hand, and I feel more creative than usual, the areas outside the box more illuminated, more obvious. And this, *this,* I remember, has to be the main reason people turn to drugs. Apparently, the military has already perfected a helmet with electrical sensors or transmitters or whatever that stimulate just the right places in the brain such that when you put it on it quiets all the competing voices in your brain and leaves you completely focussed, supremely present, and uber-confident. Supposedly puts you in that state of so-called *flow* that experts enter when performing the task that has become second nature to them after ten thousand hours of practice. The journalist who wrote the article said it completely changed her life and understanding of herself. Some crazy shit going on out there. Imagine, controlling completely your focus. Your reality is what you focus on. Can't wait to have one!

And then James, having fallen off his mad task, thank god, is asking me to show him what I'm doing. I tell him it's hard to explain and about as interesting as looking at writing in another language if you don't know it, and not any artsy language like Chinese or Arabic, or even the stern weirdness of Russian, but he insists and so I try. And, within five minutes he's bored stiff and so am I because it's not as if I'm all that interested in this either, it's just a means to an end of creating my Paul. I mean, I guess I could do it for a living if they paid me all right, but I don't want to. And I'm not going to need to. When Paul is sold for what he's going to sell for, I'm never going to have to do anything I don't want to ever again. Including die.

Unless of course some psycho strangles me in my sleep in a no-frills hotel room.

"Now let me read some more of your work," I say.

Without comment he hands me his notebook and takes another long pull of rum.

This is me relieved because he's actually writing a story now instead of his all-caps street-corner-psycho soliloquy. About the native in his cab. The writing is straight forward stream-of-consciousness and it sure ain't Tolstoy (don't ask me how I'd actually know) but there's something about it. It's about the guy the next day, who he's called Eagle Feather—that, and his choosing rum as his drink of choice says a lot about my geezer's creativity, but we can't all be idea people. Anyway, guy wakes up and remembers what happened and he prays to the creator for power and the creator hears him and grants him super strength and so he goes and finds, get this, not the two white dudes who wanted to beat him up, but the *taxi driver,* and he finds him and he tortures him (in ways that show this old man does have some creativity in him after all), but seeing's how once we hear something we never forget it, I won't burden you with the details, but he tortures him over a span supposedly of 364 years, and just before he puts him out of his misery he tells the driver, *James,* who has been pleading why why why the whole time, he tells him he's going to tell him why, and he stares at him (in his one eye he left just for this purpose) and James is dying to know (ha!) and then Eagle Feather smiles, and walks away not saying anything further, leaving James to die a slow death from the guts that are literally ripped out of him and hanging down around his feet like sausages (yep). Then, on the way to wash his hands, the creator strikes down Eagle Feather with a slow burn lightning bolt that is going to burn him alive for a thousand years in an alternate dimension.

So, yeah.

"Tell me about your kids," I try. "You lost them somehow, didn't you? Someone killed them? This is the reason for your revenge fantasy? Your fucking hating yourself? You were pickled in violence and rage and guilt and desire for revenge after

Vietnam, and all you could do was run away from it psychically afterwards, and you met your wife and had kids and she died and you were depressed again, and then they died, and now, with all the terrorism and racism it's coming up in you again, the desire to get your hands wet with blood, to get back at all the killers."

"Picasso's of Sadness," he says, softly, somewhat slurred.

"Huh?"

"Picasso's of Sadness," he says again, louder and clearer, "that's what I call them all. I'm one of them. And I do, I admit it. I long to kill someone who needs it. It's so strong, sometimes I… It was Nice, that's what really brought it back, once and for all, out of hiding. You know, the truck attack?"

"Sorta."

"How can anyone only *sorta* know about that?" he says, sounding genuinely confused. And disgusted. He gets up out of the chair at the table and looks around, takes another sip of rum, puts the bottle down, then sits back down, kicked right back with his legs splayed in front of him. Nowhere to be. He picks up the bottle again and holds it to his chest with both hands, like you might place a loved object in the hands of a corpse in a coffin. The lamp on the desk is lighting up half of him. His one eye beams even under its heavy lid.

'So, Nice," I say, because let's hear it.

"I saw the pictures, and I thought about trying to join ISIS, head over there, and from the inside kill as many of them as I could. How else to possibly deal with the brute separation of a child's foot from his leg and the blood lost and the arm crushed and the face smeared across the pavement. Every thought, every beautiful thought, every beautiful thing it added to the world, gone and never to be reassembled, turned grotesque, not ever again to be photographed and adored and loved and wondered over… covered over with a blue plastic bag and numbered and… hosed away. I'm so damn tired of forcing this faith that despite my gut I can't know and therefore have a choice. I try to choose to believe the hate isn't as bad as it appears—but what would I do for logic to actually dictate it, for it not to be forced. My mind, it's a ship in a storm and the only way I'm getting to paradise is hand firmly on the rudder, no sleep ever, keep the boat pointed, because if I let it steer itself, it's going somewhere else entirely, every wind and every wave and every current is trying to take me... That's what almost got me signing up at jihadist.com, it just felt so *right*. So unforced. Just give in to what my heart and mind and gut tell me is fucking right instead of fighting it all the fucking time."

He's not moving, but his insides are all a-rage, acid hate eating its way out at last through the final layer of its container.

"There's a jihadist.com?" I say, trying with my tone to sound funny, or at least silly. "There's a domain name that's gotta be worth a lot these days." Still nothing of course. This guy needs some serious help. He'd be the ultimate test of Pep Talk Paul. Should I have a go right now? Yeah, *sure*, maybe I could even affect a fucking Stephen Hawking voice. So I just say the only thing I can think of. "I remember seeing a picture like that, a stroller with a kid's shoe beside it." I really do, and I felt a taste of what he's talking about. I really did. I didn't even feel like that when they took my Alex away. Course, I was a different person then. A lot less capable of feeling anything. And Alex's feet and everything else are still attached. The only thing he was separated from was his sorry sad-ass mother. And according to everyone but me that was the best thing for him, so...

"I had one. A son. Three years old when Jillian died. I made a mess of it. Felt so much pressure, to not buckle, and I knew what buckling meant... At least I thought I did. The first weeks, he cried and cried for her and I stayed strong. But then he got used to it, and then I cried over that. I was *glad* he was getting used to it, so much easier, but it felt like the most wrong thing in the world, a child getting used to having no mother. My being glad about it. He grew and he grew and he grew, so smart, so capable, and I needed him to amount to something, a doctor or a lawyer or a writer, something grand, something other than a candlestick maker... something that would prove it was all worth it, that one might say it all happened for a reason... And I had done well."

"Which would speak to the quality of his mother."

"But I pushed him, and I pushed him away. He did his schoolwork, but only the minimum required, he just wanted to listen to music and ride his bike and be with friends, with girls. I hated it. I told him it was a waste, that the mind is what he needed to train, but he just wouldn't engage me on any deep level. He started competing, doing tricks on that bike of his, and actually doing well, and it just made me madder, because now it was seeming like an argument that refuted mine. And by the time he was sixteen he stopped talking to me at all. He was embarrassed of me. Taxi driver father. Who was I to talk to him of success? And he started smoking marijuana, and I ran from it, I couldn't bear it, I couldn't bear my mind telling me he was a disappointment..."

I want to jump into this pause, but what the fuck am I going to say? So I take a drink and he continues.

"And then he was going once a month to contests in the states, driving there with friends on road trips, and he got a sponsor, but it was barely enough to cover his travel and pay for his equipment. And then he had a bad crash, and he was in hospital for three days with a concussion, and I was by his side and we had some real talks, but still, I was trying to convince him to put that silly child's bike behind him, be a man, join the real world. He tried to tell me why he loved it, said it felt like flying, said it was graceful and fluid, something about poetry even, everything man strives for distilled and symbolized and simplified, finally pulling off a trick for the first time, a trick you never thought you'd get, that you've even invented. And those words, the potential in there, made me sadder than anything. What could have been! But I said nothing, and he carried on, and he admitted that it hurt him that I didn't appreciate it, didn't even try, wouldn't even come and see him do it. But I couldn't, because how could I get over the fact that compared to being something great, meaningful, it was child's play and always would be. He didn't apply himself to anything intellectual, just his bike and idiotic music and drugs and girls, which to me was just about fun. My dead wife's son. Even if he was doing it as a sport, like racing and becoming a professional, maybe being in the Tour De France, like Indurain, a training regimen that was demanding, respectable, then maybe… When I was his age…" He shifts in his chair, as if fighting gravity, but he doesn't get far. "Well, I guess I won't say things that like that around a young person like you. But, you, you know, you do remind me of him. Your wasted potential."

So, he's back to insulting me. Well, I'll be woman enough to not rise to it. *Look at me go.* But it's kind of easy, because I'm not insulted because it doesn't hit home because it's wrong. Wow, I actually *believe* that. Hmmm. Plus, I guess I'll do what I can to help this poor old geezer.

His eyes are closed and I'm pretty sure he's fallen asleep, and I'm feeling damn drunk and tired too and should probably do the same, but then he keeps going.

"Two years later he was dead. Car accident. His best friend the driver. Just driving too fast. Wrapped the car around a pole, the way they do, you know. Funny, me making my living in a car." He takes a sip. "Not even alcohol. Just stupidity and recklessness. Meaningless. Everything. I saw dead bodies in Vietnam. I made some of them dead. But seeing his broken body… May you never see your child dead. May no one ever again. His funeral, there were hundreds there. I never knew he was so popular. People who didn't even know him, just knew what he did. The friend that was driving, he tried to give a eulogy but just stood there trying, then crying, then being helped off the stage. Someone else read what he wrote, but it wasn't very good. Funny, he's one person I don't want to kill. Don't know why."

"Guess you figured he was suitably devastated."

"Maybe. Maybe."

"So you never saw him ride?"

"No, not really."

"How long ago did he…"

"November 1, 1992."

Four. I was four. I try to imagine what he looked like, basically imagine old man James here younger, and I realise he would have been really good looking. "That's way before cameras in everyone's pocket, but if he was doing well at contests there might be some YouTube of him. What was his name?"

He takes a deep breath, says, "Pablo Nunez."

I do a search.

"Find anything?" he asks, and I try and try and try but have to tell him no. "You know anything about riding bikes like that?"

Yes, I know it. Kind of, anyway. I used to love riding my bike too, remember? I remember seeing some kids doing it down at the waterfront and it was so entrancing. Me, I just rode from A to B and imagined it being A to Z. No tricks or anything, just free and easy movement, which was trick enough for me. And I know exactly what to show him, and it's so fitting yet out of our context that it feels like a backwards deja-vu or something. Like finally understanding a long ago experience.

"Okay, James. This. A friend who was a boy and not a total ass sent it to me some years ago because I loved the band that plays the song this Danny guy rides to. I didn't want to watch it because I thought it was stupid. I thought the song couldn't possibly match some guy doing tricks on a bike, I mean, it's got nothing to do with doing bike tricks, and those videos are always set to punk or death metal or whatever and I didn't want to have the song ruined. But I watched it and it's crazy moving somehow. Gets across what your boy said about it, maybe. Here, come here, let's watch it."

As if in subconscious parody of Danny, James tries to get up, doesn't make it on the first attempt, then tries again and gets to his feet, where he takes another long sip of rum and then lies down on my bed with his head up against the headboard and I give him a pillow and he puts it behind his head and I settle beside him. I try to imagine he's Danny come to rest beside me, but that's a depressing stretch, so I try to just take him for what he is, which, truth be told, is a fuck of a lot better than any man I've found myself coming up against in this life of mine so far. So I take his hand and squeeze it a little.

I turn up the volume and press play and as the arpeggiated opening chords come up and Danny MacAskill is approaching up the sidewalk, shy grin on his face, briefcase-burdened business-man walking in the background, I feel familiar shivers down my back. For about a year, every time I got really drunk or high or sad-assed I'd end up with my headphones in and cranking this fucking song and watching this and I'd imagine myself being so graceful and powerful. I haven't seen this in ages, and as the opening scene plays out, Danny pulling out the street sign that's blocking the way, jumping up on the electrical box, and trying and trying to ride the fucking top edge of a five-foot-high park railing (yep!!!) and falling and falling, *hard,* I am him. And then finally, as Ben's haunting voice holds the final OOOOOO-oooooo before the band crashes in, our hero gives it another go and he gets the front wheel along and he stops and hops and squares up the back wheel and pushes along and now he's got both wheels gliding along the top of the fence! and he slowly and jerkily glides along and he's doing it! and now he's halfway and he has to kick one leg way out for balance, a move which fifteen seconds earlier sent him painfully face-first to the ground in a tan-gle of flesh and steel, but this time the balance is just right, and he keeps gliding along and then he's on the other side and hop-ping back down to the sidewalk, defying you to imagine what it feels like, and the song proper kicks in and he sets to his set of death and gravity defying *graceful* leaps and traverses and glides that turn the normal to magic and I feel again like I want to leap out of bed and scream FUCKING *YEAH*!!! I don't look to James because I don't want to see something on his face I don't like. And I keep watching and god I love this song and this man turn-ing something ordinary as milk into physics-defying life-affirming ballet and by the end of the video, a video which starts with this dude riding the top of a fence and ends with him jumping off a bridge and riding away nonchalantly, like a bank robber trying not to be noticed, I almost have the old tears in my eyes. I sit up and look back at James, and his eyes actually are wet. He closes his eyes and I watch him and his breathing gets deeper and he falls asleep and here's to hoping he's dreaming of his son flying like a fucking bird and landing right every time.

13.

I WAKE WIDE at three a.m., as awake as if my body's never heard of sleep and only ever known feeling like right fucking shit. I'm wrung out and wrinkled, creased through with hangover sure, yes, but also because of a dream lingering in my cranial folds longer than it should. James told me about how the sea's so vicious and always has been and the Vikings used to set off on voyages with their ships only half-crewed because a bunch would always go down and they'd have to rescue and have room for the fraction of drowning mates they'd be able to pluck from the sea. But that wasn't even my dream. It was about his also telling me about the corpse collector on Greenland, sailing the coast and salvaging bodies from wrecked ships. So I dreamed I was pulling in a bloated body under the full moonlight, and no, it didn't turn out to be my boy or James or even his fucking wife or son, it was fucking me. Grotesquely distended and bursting out of my clothes, and looking...

Anyway, tell me because I want to know, how fucking stupid am I for not buying some juice or chocolate milk in preparation for this hangover drymouth? Or *eggnog*! I get up, go to the bathroom, puke. I drink three cups of water and go back to the room where James is sleeping like his life depends on it and maybe it does. I open my computer and check out the Vendée. Come on Alex! But this just makes me feel more useless and helpless and guilty. I mean, look what he's doing and look what I'm doing. Running rivers of poison through my liver and not working on my coding or bringing Paul any closer to life, with some depressed sadder-ass-than-even-me geezer lying drunkenly asleep in the cheap bed.

This is me. Wide awake in the middle of the night and in the fucking middle of a meaningless nowhere.

But *a smooth sea never a skilled mariner makes*, right?

I look it up and read that the L'Anse Aux Meadows site could have housed between thirty and one-hundred-sixty people, but they likely didn't overstay whatever meagre welcome the land offered them. There are theories that there were other sites, but no evidence of it. Looking at the map again it's almost impossible to imagine anyone doing it. I think of this other Alex out there this very moment in the wet cold, not even seasick, living his life with utmost meaning and purpose, power, direction, commitment. Danny gliding along the tops of buildings and fences. And my own Alex, not even counting on me.

"James," I say, shaking his narrow shoulder. "James. Wake up, man!"

He groans.

"We gotta go check out that village. We have to. They crossed an ocean to land here, and who are we if we let a god damn closed sign stop us. Have to be the kind of people that do the shit they intend to do. You know? *Get shit done.* I don't want to just see the sea, and rocks. I see the sea and rocks all the fucking time. I want to see the attempt at building a home, a place to live, call *home* and be happy in! Come on!"

"Okay," he says simply, then sits up and kicks his legs over. Impressive, really. Probably his army training deep in there. My trained killer.

Google satellite and the map on the PDF brochure show a restricted access road that we might be able to drive down which goes straight to the site, and even if it's gated it's only about four-hundred meters to the site, and there don't seem to be any fences other than around the site itself. We bundle up in all the clothes we have and we drive past the entrance to the park and toward the village and come to the parking with the restricted access road and turn off onto it and a sign warns us away but it's going to have to do a lot better than fucking that. There's no gate so I direct James down the road and a minute later we're at its end. He puts the car in park, sets hard the emergency brake, turns it off and we get out. It's a mostly full moon and clear and with the snow on the ground it's no problem seeing. The cold is fitting.

"Come on," I say and jump over the gate and head off down the road. It's just a few minutes and we're at the model buildings, the ruins unremarkable within the snow-dusted landscape of grass and bush and rock and the sea beyond. There's the sense of being on another planet, the moon a distant sun so far away it can't even give warmth. Feels lonely. Wholly lonelier than Alex likely feels in the cold middle of the sea. And we stand there and James says we should walk in more, explore, and I don't move, then tell him I don't think so, this is good enough. The wind is strong, smells of the sea, too much salt, seems to be telling us to go away and I feel sad. I feel like I'm staring at a graveyard where the tombstones are all gone and the bodies could be anywhere, and I guess I am and we all are, no matter where we are. Did these people go back? Feel this aloneness? Thought of home, and decided to just go back? What was the big deal that made them leave a thousand years ago anyway? Maybe they just went home. Why wouldn't they?

If you are lonely when you're alone, you're in bad company, said Sartre. But, that idea is an adaptation to a situation where we are all lonely and try to make the best of it. It's a maladaptation, isn't it? Allows us to feel okay about a society that's driving us all apart, forcing us to compete with one another and feel empty and useless. We *should* feel unhappy when we're alone, because we're supposed to be in groups, we're evolved to feel anxious and ill-at-ease when not in the presence of others. The need for company may not be cool or sexy, but it's right and fucking proper.

"Fucking desolate or what?" I say.

"I'm sure they didn't feel that way," he says, reading my goddamn mind again.

"I suppose not."

"The desolation would have made them feel that much more together."

"Cold though."

"In war, you're with brothers all the time. The ultimate unit and the ultimate experiences together. The brotherhood. The always being within earshot of friends, people who will and have killed for you. Every moment, every time you roll around in bed in the middle of the night, you hear someone coughing, or moaning, or snoring or jerking off. Always with you, like your arms and legs. You can count on them being right there with you tomorrow night. There's only one thing that could take them away, and no one can ultimately ever do anything about that anyway... And then the war ends and you come back, and you realise there was a second thing that could take them away, and you never ever feel them or that again."

We're walking back to the car when, like a part of the moon fallen to earth and drunk and staggering, what must be a flashlight in what must be someone's hand is slicing up the dark. And then it turns to us and fixes on us, blindingly.

"Hold it," says a voice behind the light and I'm about to get angry and tell them to turn the fucking light down when I remember we're trespassing.

James, I guess used to cooperating with a power more armed than he is, has stopped, and so I stop too.

We stand there unmoving, allowing the light to come closer and closer until it stops some feet away and says, "Park's closed, you know?"

"We know," I say. "We just think that taxpayers who really want to see it shouldn't have to come at a particular time of day or year."

"Yeah, well," he says, and turns the light down to our feet and comes closer. My eyes adjust and see that it's a cop—gawky and young, but intent, as though he doesn't get many opportunities to do something other than drive around and help old ladies cross the road. "All the same, I'm going to have to ticket you. Just think of it as more of your money going to help this park and this province maintain itself."

I look to James, but he's just looking at his shoes.

I'll show them fucking both. "Look, I'm from Corner Brook. This is my grandfather come to visit for the first time to Canada. All the way from Spain. He had to come here."

"I am sorry, Ma'am. But the park is closed and you both knowingly crossed the fence."

"Do you hear what I'm saying? You hear the significance? He's *Spanish*. The country of Columbus. Who was, yes, Italian, fine, but without Spain's money, he never would have got here. My gramps here, for almost his whole life he was able to say his country discovered this hemisphere. Until this place started getting headlines and he had to start acknowledging his people weren't the first to discover it, just the ones to rape and pillage it."

He takes a deep breath and exhales it through his teeth.

"Imagine if he were to go back home to his friends and tell them he got *fined* for visiting this place? It would be the ultimate insult. He'd probably have to, I don't know, fight a bull to regain his honour or something. You know the old country."

"You're really from Spain?" he says.

"Si. Gracias. Mucho Gusto," says James, with a smooth fluentness that makes him another person to me.

The copper looks at me. "All right. But count yourself lucky. My Sergeant is on us to carry through with more of these tickets. So many people trespassing here all the time."

He walks us out and to our car and James gets in and turns us around and opens the window and in English says, "Thanks a lot, eh!" and hits the gas.

Is he being cocky? Brave? Having fun? Could it be?

"That was pretty impressive," he says to me.

"Tell me about it. That was all without a low-cut top or the cleavage to make that even work."

"I'm talking more about your knowing Columbus was actually Italian."

Onward and onward we chase the darkness beyond our light. It runs from us as if luring us in, deeper and deeper, and by the time we hit Port Saunders it's past seven and dark still. The clouds have rolled in, but we only know this because of the disappearance of the stars and moon. We've been mostly silent, though James did tell me that seeing the village made him feel worse, highlighting for him how feeble we are, *feeble and transitory*. I told him I feel the same and I guess I do. I guess that's why

I'm desperate to make a mark. To give my boy a forever. Or at least respect.

"So, I told you about Alex," I say and he nods. "I told you I have access to him."

"You did," he says.

"Every four months. And next weekend is my next visit. For Christmas."

"The whole weekend?"

"Fuck no. I don't get overnights. Eleven to seven on the Saturday. And he's in St. John's. So I have to go there." I realise the way I'm saying it he probably thinks I'm about to ask him to come. Right, just what I want, I can see it now: him looking at me with pity the whole day and then forever after as well. Of course, the general set of his face is one of pity, so it wouldn't feel much different. "So I'm pretty excited about that, but nervous too. It's always bitter bittersweet."

"How could it be otherwise?"

"He lives with a middle-aged couple, mixed race, couldn't have their own kids, so they've adopted two and they foster up to two other kids at a time."

"Lucky for people like that."

"I guess… Yeah, no, you're right. And I am glad that he's got other kids around. And they do seem to love him." What the fuck am I even talking about? Why am I saying this? "Anyway, point being, this visit is set to be the least bitter and most sweet of any."

"Because of your…"

"Because it'll be my first visit where I feel like it's more than a pipedream that I'm going to get him back. Last time I kind of felt like that, but I didn't really believe it. I'd already been studying code on my own for a few months, but it still felt like a pipedream. And, understand, trying to get custody orders changed, it's very hard, seeing's how you have to prove it's in the kid's *best interests*, and my lawyer said the courts always think stability and permanency is in their best interest, so they never really want to move them around. Even back to their parents. And especially when kids are young, because they can't really know or say what they want, and they get sucked in to the new family, too. But this time, I know it's going to happen. I know I'm going to make this happen. I'm going to make my app and I'm going to be clean and the judge is going to have no choice."

It's still totally dark at 7:30, but the light's got to come soon.

"What's your timeline?" he says.

"Maybe two years. He'll be five and I hope to have him in time to start grade one wherever I decide to live."

"And where will that be?"

"Seeing's how the judge'll probably order that he have access to the foster family, at least for the first while, I'll probably be told not to go too far. But, then again, I'm going to have no problem getting around because I'll probably just get a private jet... *See?* How limited we are in our ideas when we have no money! So I don't know. Maybe try the other coast. I'd like to live in the mountains. Deep snow, you know? The kind that'll sock you in sometimes. Especially if you live somewhere remote like I'm going to. A glassy mountain chalet, a long serpentine driveway. And staff."

"So, come on. Tell me more about this app. I've told you all I've got."

Jillian. Pablo. He's even cried for me. "I just realised. Your son's name. That mean's Paul, doesn't it?"

"It does, yes."

"My app is Pep Talk Paul."

"You told me."

"Why'd you name him Paul? I just chose it because it sounds good and kind of funny with Pep Talk. And it's the male version of my name of course. Because Pep-Talk Pauline just isn't going to work, now is it? In this male dumbinated world. As if men are going to actually take life advice from a woman."

"You're probably right."

"As if probably."

"Jillian's favourite poet was Pablo Neruda. He was from Chile. I was never much into poetry and neither was she, but she figured it was auspicious to name him after a poet. I figured you can't go wrong with the Picasso connection as well."

"I suppose not."

"Yeah, well not so… Anyway, come on, tell me about your fucking Paul."

Wow. F-bomb from him! "All right, fine. It's basically…" Fuck, I'm going to have to work on my stupid elevator pitch. "You know lifestyle gurus, self-help books selling zillions, yes-men, professional *pep-talkers*?"

"I suppose."

"Well imagine an app, basically an AI, artificial intelligence, that works like your own personal pep-talker. Except he doesn't give you standard slogans about living in the moment and not sweating the small stuff and that kind of mundane dollar store shit. No, he helps you convince yourself of anything you want to believe. Like, imagine the best debater in the world, the best lawyer, fighting for you, their job only to help you understand what you want and why you should do it. You know, like law's so grey that the difference between guilt and innocence is a good lawyer, like that, but for your life and morals and everything and anything. Like, let's say I want to move to France, it'll give me all the good reasons why I should. It's about justifying what you want to do, and also making you feel better about the bad things in your life. Like, I don't know, and remember, I myself don't totally understand it yet, but it'll come. Like you want to buy a new car but your gut tells you you should donate the money instead."

"A Ferrari."

"Exactly. Paul will tell you you deserve that car, that the donations won't make a difference anyway, that you work hard for your money, that we pay taxes to help people that need help-ing, it's not necessary to give extra, that the purchase will stimu-late the economy and that ultimately helps everybody more, that new cars are more fuel efficient so it's better for the environment, that new cars are safer for kids, whether they be in the back seat or behind you when you're backing up with a camera to see them, that charity only makes man weak, that smooth seas never make skilled sailors… Like that."

"Hmmm," is what he says.

"Right now I'm kind of just collecting quotes. You know, you're feeling lonely and you look up quotes on loneliness and it's not too long before you find one that makes you feel better. Like music does. It'll be kind of like that, but much more specific and dynamic."

"So, if I want to go out and kill a bunch of people but feel bad about it, Paul will help me feel good about it?"

"I know people are going to say that... But, well yes, basically, if it's what you truly want to do, then Paul'll sort you. But, as Paul gets more refined and intelligent and gets to know you better, he's only going to convince you of things you *actually* want to do, and odds are that in your heart you don't actually want to kill them, you want to forgive them and put it behind you and maybe even convert that to love. Except for psychopaths, who don't need a PTP anyway, at heart all people want love and respect and community, they just, a lot of them don't know how to go about getting it."

"So when Paul is smart enough it'll basically prove we're all the same and there is a standard morality?"

"*No.* That's not what, no. Obviously not."

"But, that's what you're—"

"Fuck, whatever. And if you do really want to kill someone, then you *should*, as long as you know the consequences. And maybe regulators will put in safeguards like Paul can't convince people to kill others, or blow up buildings or whatever. Like Assimov's rules for AI, though it's accepted that those are pure entertainment and actually meaningless and a much more vigorous system's got to be made."

"Well that is interesting.'

"I can't explain it well, but it's a lot more than what I've said. It's going to be revolutionary."

"You sure you can build it?"

"No one person can build the complete thing. The power of Google or whoever is going to have to do that. I just have to do enough to demonstrate proof of concept, get a basic version working reasonably well, show its potential, and then, well, everyone and their yappy dog thinks they're going to score some of Google's googolplex of bucks, but..."

He doesn't say anything more and I'm sure he's fighting his fatherly response to tell me it'll never work.

"Like my online teacher told us. Aps don't have to make money for you to sell them for a lot, they just have to collect data on people. And imagine how much data PTP will collect on people. Their most private deepest thoughts and wishes!"

"It'll never work," he says.

"I'm glad I can trust you to speak your mind."

"People don't work that way. And the level of intelligence the thing would have to have, well…"

"Yeah, well, you're not exactly up on the modern world now are you? What do you know about computers or AI or anything like it?"

"Granted. But…"

I'm glad he doesn't say anything more about that, because I don't want to have to get mad at him.

"Another problem is that if it were able to work as you describe, well, it would ruin civilization. A world where everyone just does what they want and feels justified? Imagine. A world of gluttons."

"How would it be a world of gluttons any more than this piece of shit world is now? And if people start to feel better about themselves maybe they'll start to be nicer, less desperate, less vicious. The real danger is that it'll turn everyone into a bigot. You know, he who knows only his side of the argument barely knows that. Well, it's going to be that times ten, but I'll sleep fine at night because the tipping point's already been reached and humanity's ruined already and further ruination is likely inevitable and if I can make a bunch of money off it, you better believe I'm going to so I can hopefully be one of those above it all. And I'll make up for being a shitty mom."

"That's pretty hopeless."

"*You're* the one who wants to kill and then kill himself. Don't try to tell me it's to be a saint or a martyr. It's just more gluttony. That's what all your writing is. Drunken indulgence. Paul *could* potentially save the world."

He falls silent and so the fuck be it. The sky's lightening now and we're passing through Gros Morne, not that you can see any of it. "But I guess I do, James. I hope and I think it will uncover a universal morality in everyone. That makes the most sense to me. It sits in my gut. Maybe it'll save us all."

"Sounds like faith. Religion, even."

"Sure, whatever. Maybe it'll be like a Jesus. Maybe it's *actually* Jesus Christ. Bible never said what form he'd exactly take when he came back."

"Well, Pauline, that really is ambitious. And I support you in it. You have to follow your dreams, right."

"Nice try, James. But I'm not your kid, and you're too old to be changing your ways now."

He actually *laughs*. Says he guesses I'm right.

And I've actually just blown myself away. Maybe PTP *is* going to be Jesus. And that would make me...

The sky's light now and I can see him clearly, that which isn't covered by this black hair anyway. Must be so nice to be so hairy, cover up all your trouble skin and double chin, even your lips, just be a big hair ball. I watch him as he drives the car, so confident, likes it's an extension of him. I wonder how many hours of practice he's put in. Probably way more than the old ten-thousand hours they say you need to perfect something. Not like he's driving a race car or anything, but he certainly does it with measured calm, grace, and you have the sense that the last thing he's going to do is make a mistake. Not often you feel that way with someone. I imagine him behind the wheel of a ship, of Alex's Boss Benz. That's what Alex looks like, at one with that mighty graceful machine, riding that razor edge of speed and progress amongst forces that would crush it. I imagine his Pablo, the pro BMXer that hated his father, how he must have looked like that. And I picture Danny riding the top edge of that fence like a cat on a bike, kicking his leg out and holding it together and keeping the wheels moving and pulling off his beautiful miracle. And I think about that *Flow* machine the military is perfecting, how maybe it will help people achieve such skill and grace almost overnight. And with a perfected PTP, you can almost picture a world you'd want to live in. People you'd want to be around.

Perhaps even yourself.

14.

St. John's. Seeing's how this is where my son was stolen away to, you might guess I have some mixed feelings about this place, and if you did you'd be wrong: I fucking hate that he's here and I hate coming here and my feeling about it all is firm and fixed. My body gets tenser and tenser the closer I get, and the buildings loom like thugs waiting to pounce and the lights are all laser beams aimed at my brain's deepest pain centers. I have a couple friends here, but I never see them. I never see anyone anymore. Point being I'm sat at the bar at O'Reilley's pub by myself, receiving no attention from anyone other than the bartender who's paid to give it, and I'm trying to not get so drunk that I'm hung over tomorrow. You might also guess I'd be excited, desperate for the minutes to fly by as fast as physics allows for, but again, fucking wrongo. And it would be obvious that either you have no kids or you've at least never had said kids stolen from you and then had to visit them. I'm always scared shitless, which you probably now realise you would be too.

One visit every four months, and if it's no good, that's my kid's memory of me for his next four months, which to a three-year-old is the equivalent of like four years. Four fucking months, one-twelfth of his entire life in between visits, equivalent to two and a half years if he were my age. He spends .003% of his days with me, his mother. Yes, I'm good at math, maybe my only natural talent. Point being, it's a lot of fucking pressure, and it's only going to get worse as he gets older. And the whole fucking day I'm fighting back tears as I think of how much I love the little guy and can't believe I don't get to do this every day like normal parents and how fucked is that and god how fucking sad can anything be? How can anyone have the authority to take your *child* from you? And I think about whether these foster parents are actually child molesters raping my sweet child every night because you never fucking know, it happens, and that's two people I'm going to have to figure out how to murder someday. Oh, and on top of all that, imagine what it feels like to have your own kid make strange with you when he sees you. Bet you can't even imagine what that would feel like if your dog did it, never even mind your kid! And then there's the fact of every day of the four months between visits you're thinking about how that very day your kid is falling helplessly in love with a fucking stranger named fucking Francine and you're fading even fucking farther from his mind and heart. And just wait till he hits his teen years and starts fucking hating you for having him because he's so fucked up.

"Sir. Another, please!" I yell at the tender and he acknowledges me with a nod. I'm drinking rum. Yep. And straight too. Gotta keep the calories down! I'm down three pounds this past month! Not fucking bad, eh?!

At least it's not as bad as when I had supervised visits at Protection Services. Not that they watched me too closely, it's not like I ever abused Alex, just supposedly neglected him, put him at risk of harm through my drug use, and put him at risk of further emotional and physical harm when I was being beaten up by his fuck of a father. Seeing's how it's all true I admit it, but they didn't need to take him away from me! And if I were as rich as I'm going to be and could afford a kick-ass lawyer I'm sure he'd be living with me right now. Course if I was rich I'm sure none of the other shit would have happened either. But, whatever, here I am. And on fucking *Durdle* Street is he, and tomorrow we'll meet for a brief time, and then we'll part again, and I'll deal with it by knowing that I'm not going to be doing this forever. No way, no fucking how. And to that end, I need to get out of this place and get fucking to my hotel room and do some work on Paul.

I'm right the fuck early as always—you never know when you're going to get a flat or a blown carburetor-or-whatever or t-boned by a texting truckdriver, so I always give myself lots of time because even though I know he's too young to have any idea of actual clock time, other than high the last thing I'm going to be is late. So I pull into the parking lot of his school, Goulds Elementary, which he started in September. He's not even four yet, as his birthday is December 30 (yep, that makes this visit a Christmas *and* birthday visit with him—no pressure, right?), but he has started *school*. I park in a spot across from a window to a classroom—not his, given the work I can see on the walls, obviously of kids older than him. The work is sheets of paper with a kid's drawing of his mother and his favourite things about her. Well, I can't tell what this work is exactly, but you know somewhere in this school there's a damn display with something like that on it. Some dip-shit know-nothing sees-her-ma-'n-pa every fucking weekend skinny blonde chickie teacher so happy with her so happy and satisfying life... Maybe he visits this classroom, for a reading mentor or something, I don't know. Why would I know, I'm only his mother, right? Either way, it's surreal to be sitting outside the school that *my son* attends. I never even had the chance to take him to school on his first day. Fuck, I never even had him long enough to get used to the idea that I had a son or was a mother.

All right, fine. I have to stop saying that, don't I? I need to start taking some fucking responsibility for this. It's true, I fucked him over. He may be doing wellish now, but there are seeds in that little brain, poisonous little seeds that hopefully, by the good grace of his foster parents and my awakening will never be further watered and so will eventually die and decompose and be gone completely. But they're there, planted by me. Good ole fucking me. Good parents never plant any poison seeds in their kids' brains. Would never dream of it. Would do anything in their power to not do it. But the only dreams I was having at that time were nightmares and I swear I didn't know what I was doing. And I promise that's not an excuse, it's an explanation. And I do, I accept responsibility. I do. This is me, mea culpa. I will never again say he got taken from me, I will rub my nose in my own shit and I'll call it like it is—he got *rescued*. I couldn't protect him so someone else did. My Alex got *rescued* from his fucked mother and useless cunt father (until that asshole accepts some responsibility he gets no mercy and no reprieve). And if *he* ever actually does come forward claiming to want to play some role in Alex's life I'll fight that fucker like a pissed off cat who's just completed master-class training with an industrial paper shredder.

And if I have to, I'll sic my geezer former and wanna-once-again-be killer on him.

Fuck, I don't know if I can *do* this anymore. Jesus *H*. Paul!

The only mistake to regret is the one you don't learn from.

I can't believe you're fucking quoting my *mother!* And fuck, man, I fucking *used hard fucking drugs,* while he was a defenseless fetus completely dependent on me, prisoner in my body! And then to still use even after he was taken from me and told I had to stop to get him back! To still even be using now! What kind of useless piece of shit!

You had your reasons. You were depressed and physically and emo-tionally abused. You said yourself you weren't going to let anyone judge you for how you responded to that shit, and now here you are judging yourself again. You're through with that, remember? You did what you had to to survive, to cope. And you did. And you're making up for it now. If you hadn't done that then, you might be dead for all you know. And Alex too.

You buy that shit? You think that's fair? Fine, I was being beaten up. I was alone. I had no one, but to use while pregnant. It's the lowest of the fucking low!

Only good people feel guilt. And no one knows what it's like. Not the judge, not the foster parents, not anyone but you. Rock bottom has become the solid foundation upon which you are rebuilding your new life. *Remember that one? Rowling? Without going through this you wouldn't be the person you are now. You couldn't be the perfect mother you are soon to be.* Hardships prepare ordinary people for an extraordinary destiny.

Nice try. The proper quote throws 'often' in there. Sometimes hardships just destroy people. And *destiny*? As fuck-ing if.

Just look how changed you are already!

But have I, that much? Look at me. Still using sometimes. Almost *casually,* with James!

Well, you never will again. That was the last time. The fact that it was casual is super meaningful. You're not addicted at all. You're just using for something to do now. That's huge.

But is it true?

Make it true.

Yeah, sure. Can just imagine what the judge would have to say to me if he knew.

To hell with the judge. He won't know, and it doesn't matter. The next time you're in front of him it will have been years since you used. And you're going to be before him all fit and trim and beautiful with a bank account full of money, and he's going to have no choice.

Yeah, sure, unless I fuck up this visit. And the next one. And Alex keeps growing further and further apart from me, and then I probably won't even believe that he's best off being returned to me.

Okay, now you're just getting ridiculous. Come on, stop thinking like this. Fucking hell.

…

So I guess we'll just leave it there, eh? Christ, Paul, I better hurry up and get the real you working, because this only-me version of you really sucks.

I'll try not to take that personally.

Any fucking way, it's time to go. So here I go.

Here I go.

Pulling out of the parking lot of his school.

Careful careful careful check both ways and check again. Turning left on Doyle's Road, then right on Main, past the Mary Browns, the Pharmacy Solutions, then the very first right on Durdle. *Durdle.*

So careful. Brain surgery. Not as careful even as I'll drive when he's in the car because I will never hurt him again.

Up fucking Durdle with all its slightly varied but ultimately identical vinyl-sided shoebox-shaped detached houses. But they're not are they? Every one of them houses a selection of people as unique and different from one another as things can be. How different each of their stories. How varied the mistakes they've made, and continue to make, and the ways in which they try and fail to make up for them. I stop in front of the vomit green one, the only one that matters, with the circa seventies camper in the driveway that makes me so sad every time as I think of getting behind the wheel with Alex in the passenger seat and a whole whack of time and space stretched out before me to do whatever I wish in and I shut 'er down right there. *I will not do this anymore.* I will earn it back and more. You might want to fucking just wait and see (and you have, haven't you!).

I look at the living room window, hoping as always to see her standing there holding him and making him wave to me, but there's no one there.

These little things. Tell me you wouldn't, if you were a foster mother with any heart at all, if you actually wanted to make the mother feel fucking special or even just welcome, *anticipated, considered, involved, not insignificant,* you'd be fucking standing at the window with her son and jumping up and down enthusiastically and saying *mom's here mom's here yay!!!* or some such encouraging shit??! But nope, just an empty fucking window.

But I deserve all this. This is to be endured and gotten through. *If you're going through hell, keep going,* right?

I ring the bell and Francine comes, looking harried, and I ignore the part of my brain that tells me she does it on purpose, that she's trying to tell me my son's a right fucking brain-damaged handful and that's why she won't adopt him and if I had any decency at all she would never have had to have been in this position.

That I should at least have the decency to just leave him be after all I've done to him.

"Come on in," she says without a hello never mind a hug, because after all why would she hug me, why would she want Alex to see her hugging me? "Sorry, we're a little behind schedule. Bruce is supposed to be home by now. Just wait here a sec and I'll get him," she says, and heads off around the corner and out of sight, because why would Alex's real mother have any interest in coming to see his room, the things he chooses to have on the walls, the toys he opts to play with, the space in which he fucking exists. Make sure there are no bars and chains and whips and blood stains and video cameras and *fuck!*

I listen out for any sound and hear nothing and so I close my eyes and try to devote every neuron usually engaged in seeing to hearing, any sound of him… and then, there! Him! Sound waves called into being by his sweet vocal cords, travelling through the ether and lapping up on the shores of my ear drums, so beautiful and so sweet and so perfect. And I bask in the sound that gets louder and louder, no words, just mumbling, not actually perfect at all, and then I open my eyes and there he is, holding Francine's hand, standing up almost to her hips now, so big and small at the same time. His gigantic-little hand in hers, and he's looking up at me and his gigantic-little feet are hesitating and he's pulling back.

"I know, I'm sorry. It's long, but he cries and cries when we try to cut it," she says, about his hair I guess.

"Has he got any words yet?" I say, keeping it together, trying to understand that it's completely normal and even a 'good' sign that he's not rushing to greet me with arms open wide and yelling MOMMY!!

"No, not really. He's got mama, but it's probably not even related to me, just the sound that's easiest to make."

Of course I cringe at that, but I don't buckle, because she's right. My son's got a problem with speech and we'll see what happens with it. Whatever happens with it while he's here, what's going to happen with it when he's with me is it's going to be fucking fixed even if I have to fund my own lab and team of scientists to work on it.

She's not offering him up and tell me cause I want to know wouldn't you want to fucking wrap your hands around her throat and squeeze until she's done breathing because is she even fucking human and if the state has seen fit to place your child in the care of a non-human what the hell else are you going to do but solve that particular problem and just deal with whichever one the fucking shit-ass state deals you next. But seeing's how doing that's obviously not going to get me any fucking closer to actually having my child back, I ignore her and get down on my knees and open my arms wide and try to banish all the fucking hurt and pain and worry from my face and replace it all with excitement and happiness and warmth, and start engraving my Academy award because it fucking works! He comes to me, smile on his perfectly perfectly perfectly flawlessly perfect face and he puts his arms stiffly around my head and I hug him so tight and breathe in so deeply of his scent and try my best to make the moment stop and stop and stop and stop and stop.

He's in the car seat to the rear and right of me and I make sure I keep my eyes on the road, but of course I'm watching the rear-view mirror and noticing his swiveling beautiful head and darting beautiful eyes and the way he reaches for things out of reach and points and grabs... and makes no intelligible sounds. And finally far enough away to feel safely alone I stop the car and pull to the side of the road and take him out of his car seat and hold him tight and open the front passenger side door and slide into the seat and hug him so hard and he wrestles with me and he starts crying and I want to cry too but I don't, and I don't let him go.

The aquarium was great, he loved it. I mean loved it. And I got such great pictures of us. A shark of course, and the lava-lamp-like jellyfish, and all the rest. Hundreds. Enough to last the next four months. No, he didn't choose any of these moments to break through his dam of silence and speak for the first time because he so desperately needs to tell me he loves me and misses me so much and wants to come home to me and to bring his matter back to court and tell the judge all this so that he can finally be happy.

Maybe fucking next time.

And then we went to the mall and I pushed him around in a mall stroller and let him walk when he wanted to and in the Disney store his favourite thing was the Star Wars stuff which was highly disappointing while also being highly reassuring—such is the way of this world we've made for our children, I guess—and then we went for dinner at the Jack Astor's. And that's where it all went downhill, fast of course. Which is to obviously say you better not expect a play-by-play account of it here, because I'm not about to torture myself. Point being he had a tantrum for no apparent reason and I did everything I could think of to contain it—which basically consisted of trying to reassure him and then offer him the toys I had with me and then offering every piece of food I'd ordered, but nothing calmed him. And forget not being able to talk, in his whines and moans and screams he expounded eloquently on every fucking shit aspect of my exis-tence and character.

Until... yep, you guessed it. I gave in and called Francine. And listened to her as she reassured me that 'this' 'happens' 'sometimes' – though 'she' 'can't' 'remember' 'the' 'last' 'time' 'it' 'did'. And she asked me to put the phone by his ear and I did and I closed my eyes and imagined I was in a different time and place and body and reality and body and his crying and writhing stopped and I put the phone back to my ears and imagined I was James vocalizing his writing but was actually just silent listening to Francine tell me he'll be fine and I should probably think about, if I had nothing else 'important' (I kid you not!) planned with him, bringing him home now. And god damn how I didn't want to. Fucking fucking fucking didn't want to and I shouldn't shouldn't shouldn't have.

And you might want to think about not saying a fucking thing. Especially seeing's how when I got home I realised I hadn't even given him his Christmas slash birthday present. And she never reminded or even asked about it. As if she never expected me to even bring him one.

15.

THERE THEY GO, their little arrows. In their little boats, just setting off on their way across the Indian Ocean. The comfort of Australia above them for a while, but no contact, and then the whole of the South Pacific to get across, an ocean of cold ocean, a tidal wave of waves. The way home. Their sweet little way. *Little.* Imagine being on the deck of their ship, see how little it all feels. See if anything has ever felt less little in your whole little life. Imagine months spent trying to cross this lurching howling wind-molested expanse of deep cold heaving sun-starved sea. Imagine the time looming.

Like the vast expanse of time looming ahead of me before I see my boy again. What gales and rogue waves lie in wait, trying to prevent me from ever seeing him again. Seems like an impossibility.

My son. Poor. Fucking.

How much older he's going to be. How much more distant from me. How much more of a shell I shall be to him. How much harder to break through, if I can at all.

Will he actually be speaking by then? God, please.

One of the sailors, the Japanese, Koji, has broken his mast. His back.

Is that me? Is that my metaphor?

No fucking way.

I've got no cracked spine or any other impediments. I'm whoever ends up winning.

Just watch and see me go.

"I don't know the words," I tell him. "I don't want to be melodramatic, but, maybe I need to hop on a bike, set it to some perfect music, ride into an oncoming car. Seeing's how…"

He says nothing. Doesn't come to me, attempt to hug me. Just sits at the dining room table with his legs crossed and his head against his fisted hand, arms propped up on the table. Drunk.

"I dropped him off and he *ran* to her. Just short of desperate. Hugged her and let himself be held by her as though he'll never cry again. Then Bruce comes, gives me a quick hello and a ridiculously boisterous hello to Alex, like he's trying to win the Oscar for best supporting actor in the role of fantabulistic-fuck-ing-foster-father-that-makes-the-bitch-druggie-biomother-feel-like-a-pitiful-tit by acting like the young boy is the first young boy he's ever seen and he's afraid he might be the last and he doesn't want to disappoint him. And foster mother, she…"

I take a long pull of my beer. Then another. He's still just sitting there, if anything laying himself even flatter into his chair.

"I told her about my plans. Told her I'm not going to be applying for status review this time around because… I just told her I'm busy studying and it's probably going to be two years, but it's going to be successful and I just want her to be prepared for that. And I promised I'll always let her see Alex. And what does she do? Tell me you want to fucking know! She rolls her eyes! Well, she didn't, really, not really, but she *did*. It was so fucking clear; she thinks I'm just making up excuses. And she points out that I've lost weight and she supposedly knows what that means. And she can't imagine what torture it is, but maybe I should just accept what I cannot change, know that my son's got a good forever home, and put it behind me. And I was so fucking mad the only thing I could do was walk away."

Apparently he's got nothing to say to even that. How do you say nothing to that? When you lost your own son? Jesus H, I feel like I'm falling apart here. Koji on his fucking boat with the mast cracking in the middle of the night. Is there no one in this whole insanely large insanely cold universe that gives a shit, that thinks of me before themselves?

Finally, "Must be really hard," he says lamely. And the award for psychiatrist of the year goes to, drumroll…

Survival brain says change the subject. *Change the fucking subject!* I look around this place, this home to someone we've never even met. "Don't you find it at all hypocritical, that you stay in an Airbnb space, while you say it's Uber that forced your hand to retire before you can actually afford to?" This is me trying.

"This is the world. The only way we survive is by sacrificing our morals and once everyone's done that no one has to feel bad about doing and taking whatever they want. You don't even have to hate people so much anymore."

"You're no fucking Pep Talk Paul, you know?"

"That's for you to build. Immaculate conception, remember?"

"Too easy, James," I say. "You ass. Too fucking easy."

"I never said I was anything other than human."

"Definition of," I say, getting up to leave. "Time to set the bar a little higher."

16

JESUS H. I'M blocked like a glacier. The big ideas frozen up, just enough melt water for me to remain conscious that I'm still alive. Because this idea is fundamentally flawed? Because *I'm* fundamentally flawed?

No.

Learn code. And code and code. Get better. And better and better. Work on your assignments and it's going to come!

But I can't focus. It's only two thirty and I'm trying to stay up till at least 10 a.m. for Christ sakes! I had big plans for this night! It's Christmas day. Meeeeeeeeeeeeeerry Chris-moss!

I head up to the flat section of the roof where I go sometimes to look over the harbour, and I sit with my bottle of rum and look up and imagine Santa flying by. There isn't a single sign of life. Not one. Only my blooms of breath. There aren't even stars overhead. Or even sounds. I guess this is as dead as the world gets, 2:37 a.m. on Christmas morning on top of a house in Cornerbrook. Except in houses there is life. That's where life goes to live itself in private, to lay low, amongst its kind. There are creatures stirring, mice. There are kids staying up in their rooms, waiting to hear Santa Clause, full of wonder that this is the night he comes, and if they just stay up long enough they'll actually hear him! But they're filled with doubt, because they know they can't stay up that long—to a child all-night's an ocean, impossible to cross alone. But, there are songs in which kids encounter Santa, so there is hope.

Alex is asleep. He's too young to have any control over waking and sleeping.

Seeing's how I'm an idiot, my mind goes to James. Says go to him. Expect nothing, but at least be in the company of another.

No way.

Look at the water. So dark. Darker than space. Thicker and colder. Picture the other Alex out there trawling along the basement of the Pacific. The same gravity that holds this water in place, holding his whole Southern Ocean in place. Some semblance of. Under me. I put myself out on the cold water out there. I imagine being in a canoe, and it splits in half and leaves me to float on my own. Those skippers, this is what they contend with. At any moment they might be divested of their ship and left alone in the middlest and wettest of nowheres. And they try not to think about it, but at any moment it could happen. It has and will again. Any minute now. Ram a random shipping container and there goes your boat. Your warmth gone, likely even your life. Our bodies are those boats and we're all in them. Any second our heart could ram up against an immoveable object and leave us in the middlest of nowheres. Windless and sinking. It will. It is written. Written and written.

But we will escape this. Some of us. The singularity. We can live forever. Some of us. This is being written.

If we are communally minded, doesn't that make it worth the loss of most of us? *Love.* The love you have for your child so pure not because he's your child, your blood, you, nothing narcissistic like that—it's pure through and through and beautiful. It's because you see that there is nothing detestable in this child, pure and uncynical, unegotistical experiment and response, joy. The love you have for him is untainted by jealousy or spite or fear or anything at all negative; it's the only pure thing you know, and once you've tasted such purity you are different, your world is different, and there's nothing you won't do to maintain it. You are responsible for this and you are committed and there is nothing holding you back and it is absolute and it is scary. If someone takes if from you, you are destroyed. And you will destroy.

Even if you were a fucking idiot and didn't realise it until it was too late.

Crucial correction: *Almost* too late.

Back at my desk I stare at my phone, doing its long-ago perfected impression of rigor mortis and I know there will be no further communication this night. And that's good. This girl's never had a problem with being alone.

My finger guides the cursor to the Vendée site and I click on it. And on that site I discover that if I click the name box beside the little arrow representing the boat I get a three-hundred-sixty degree VR of the boat in its current conditions, such that I can fly around it like a drone, as it crashes through the waves or the calm, the sunlight or the moonlight or the dark, and with sound! The gentle splash of those like Alex in lighter winds, or the blustery roar of those in a heavy system, like JP Dick, with surf crashing and wind whistling. It's like I'm there. I sit and hover above JP's boat and watch and imagine, and then I close my eyes and listen and it's even easier to imagine. And I think about him and them all, out there still in the world, exactly in their place and doing what they have to do, everything they have to and nothing they don't. Tough. Focussed.

And that has to be me. Come *on!* I'm a woman with a child in the care of the queen of England and I've got an app to build that's going to change the world, change the functioning of humanity, maybe render politics and psychology games that are finished.

I open up another browser and search some quotes, sailing related, and find one from Pete Goss: "The Cancer of time is complacency. If you're going to do something, do it now. Tomorrow is too late." I like the time as cancer metaphor, but we've all heard it before. I broaden my search and come up with something more up my alley: "If you don't have the mental capacity to be obsessed about what you're trying to get... then motherfucker you ain't never gonna have it."

Exactly fucking right. Time to get obsessed.

The End.

FINE. YOU'RE ONE of those people who hate books that end without having things spelled out for you, or whatever. Because I'm that kind of person I'll tell you a little more. Like an encore, I guess. And since you're just going to Google it anyway, I might as well let you hear it from me in my words. So here you go. Or *fine*, maybe *I* can't let *you* go. Whatever. Right?

So:

James and I kept up our whatever-you-call-it through January 19th, the day Armel beat my beleaguered but not-dispirited Alex by a mere sixteen hours to win the Vendée, and through the next weeks as sailors dribbled into port I kept serving people their booze-laden drinks to special-up their moments, working on my courses, and trying not to think too much about my April visit to my Alex.

James was still working on his message in a bottle, drinking more for sure, which was obvious in his walk and his gaze, a light in his eyes dimming or receding. He called me over to his table on a rainy Valentine's day afternoon on the way to PAB, and as I looked at him I couldn't but worry, seeing's how it seemed some light had been switched off deep within him.

"Know where Destremau is today?" he said.

"He's turned back?"

I felt like that was a pretty funny answer, but he looked disappointed. Not, I think, because I was annoying him with such a response, but because he actually wanted to be able to say that something absurd like that did happen. Something beyond just simply, 'simple', sailing?

"It's an even hundred days at sea today," he said, and I don't know if he even realised it was Valentine's day, even despite the stupid decorations I had to put up. "Eric Bellion got in yesterday. Destremeau's just off the hip of South America now."

He had told me it was the last finishers that impress him the most, as they had the hardest time but still finished, that it's all about how hard the challenge that they overcome. "Well, they're all out of the Southern Ocean so likely all safe now, right?" I said, hoping to impress him with my knowledge.

"A lot of ground for him to cover though. Lots of flotsam and jetsam."

"What the fuck exactly is flotsam? And what distinguishes it from jetsam?" I said, to be difficult.

"Jetsam's what gets tossed overboard on purpose, flotsam's what you tried to save but couldn't."

I felt like I walked into that. Can't believe he actually knew. "Hmmm. So when's he projected to finish?"

"Another month or so."

"Then they're all in?"

"Yep, all of them."

Yes, it was there. In his tone, something. He was hoping for adventure, something beyond ho-hum everyone-finishing, some need for a rescue, at least some cause for worry. Like the race would be meaningless without it and that depressed him. Course, what didn't? The straight-forwardness of this modern race offended him; castrated arc—though it's still hard, it's not dangerous enough. He'd prefer to have been witness to the older ones, where communication was such that weeks went by without even being sure your guy was still on the surface of the water, still alive and breathing. Not knowing where they were, *if* they even were any longer. I think he was actually hoping to have someone die out there, someone for him to feel continually at one with, for him to keep always thinking about being out there alone, rather than living their lives in the real world after landing.

He also said something else, told me that Crowhurst, the guy who tried to fool everybody in the first race and walked off his boat, and Tetley, another almost finisher of that original race, on March twenty-fourth in the middle of the Atlantic came so close together that they likely would have seen one another if it hadn't been for stormy seas and low visibility. All those thousands of miles and hundreds of days, to actually end up in the same place at the same time, especially when one of them wasn't even going around the world. He said it just amazed him. And how if they actually had seen one another and said a hello, who knows, Crowhurst might not have killed himself. Was he suggesting our meeting was just as crazy and unlikely and therefore special? That maybe I'd saved him or vice-versa? No—he went on to say it shows how alone we really all are, no matter how close we get to people. Yep, my geezer. Maybe he wanted me to argue. Maybe he was that desperate.

Or maybe that's just all me writing with the benefit of hindsight. Imagining what wasn't there, imagining and needing my James to be something deep and significant and outside the normal run of things.

Anyway, whatever that was all about, something distinctly outside the normal run of things happened when we were three hours from PAB, almost *exactly* half-way across and farthest from port. I heard a commotion, a flurry of my gods and then calls for help and it turned out that it was my James, having collapsed from his seat and onto the hard pile carpeted floor. And I'm ashamed, I guess, to say I froze, because us staff are all trained to provide first aid, given that the ferries don't have nurses or obviously doctors on board. But thankfully it didn't matter because one of the people that got to him first *was* a nurse and was able to give him CPR and revive him and keep him vived until the helicopter arrived to whisk him away, which was all quite a sight for crew and customers alike. But for me, well, I still don't even know how to describe what it was. I can tell you that I tried to tell the paramedics that I was a friend of his and wanted to go with him, but they said they couldn't take me.

So as I watched the helicopter take off through the window, I imagined a smile on James's face, as he imagined himself being evacuated by huey after being shot through the lung in some rice paddy in Vietnam. A hero being rescued, finally getting to live as a hero, even if it means dying.

So, yeah, I pictured him happy and heroic. '*Poetic*'. And that's where the story should end, him dying on that chopper with all his beautiful happy-making delusions intact at the final moment and therefore an eternity of sorts. A heaven. But no, they kept him alive and brought him to QEII Health Sciences in Halifax, where when I got there they told me he had a heart attack and stroke and I went to see him every day for the first four days of his unconsciousness, feeling like an anchor had been pulled for both of us. Or set. Fucking stroke. Probably all the neuronal connections that made him who he was were now cut. Every memory and conception of his wife, his son, his hate, me, now cut, like a spider web vacuumed up. A net that's all hole.

And then something in him lets go and dies. With me sitting right beside him, he fucking dies. No grand awakening, opening of the eyes, squeezing of my hands as I hold him and accompany him across to wherever the fuck. He just dies in his sleep and shits his pants and good for him I guess.

The coroner and the city officials, unable to find any relatives on the ID they had, and content that I was a girlfriend to him, given the proof I was able to provide of our trip to LAM, were happy to leave the 'arrangements' to me. And ever so helpfully there was funeral home guy there to see me, and he showed me the packages and I told him to go to hell and I went to another scurvy funeral parlour in town and bought the cheapest package known to man in this corner of the world and thank god for my new credit card with its twelve grand limit I got since starting this job. No big bleeding heart heroism on my part—before long this amount of money is going to be the equivalent of buying a cup of coffee. And I opted for cremation of course and I thought of making another quilt, another collection of holes, and pressing his ashes into the fibers but that's not him and it's most certainly not fucking me.

I thought of putting him in an urn behind the bar, maybe in an empty booze bottle and fuck do I love that idea, talk about a message in a bottle, and it would work if I was a tender in anything other than a federally regulated liquor dispensation facility on a sea-faring vessel serving the public, on which every inch is accounted for and cleaned on a regular basis. Even if I sprinkled a bit of him on the bar or behind the dishwasher there would at least then always be a particle of him around, no matter how thorough the cleaning. But, in the end, keeping in mind that idea that every breath you take you breathe in a few atoms of Jesus H, it seemed insulting and it grossed me out.

Of course I thought of his talk of his wife's grave, somewhere out there a headstone waiting all these years to have his date of demise hacked into it, the completion of an equation, but nothing in me felt any connection to that. I guess despite what I told him I just don't think a woman who knew the him of all those years ago would really want this him of now. And surely, if she's somewhere up there, she's found someone else by now!

I got his journal and I looked in it, and I guess since letting me read it he'd taken to rewriting over his past writings, since they were meaningless anyway, he said, and so his journal was illegible, just one line written over another, just a mess of overwritten black pencil, like a killing field of dismembered, mushed up black ants, body parts lined up row by row. You'd think there'd be one line, one last line, like with instructions or words of thanks or love of something or something, but no, right down to the last line it seems he never put pencil down until the last thing he wrote was obscured enough.

I guess he knew he wasn't long for this world. Probably some months before getting on my ferry he was told by his doctor that if he doesn't stop drinking, doesn't stop with the sadness and anger over everything, he's going to die, and I imagine a light bulb going off over his head and the plan instantly forming in his head—delve into the hate and anger, light it on fire with booze every day, ride the ferry back and forth and fight the good fight till you die. At sea. Like a 'man'. On the front lines and facing forwards.

I wear his watch now. Got it fixed and it tells changing time once again after all these years, though something made me set it five minutes slow. And I put some of his ashes in the body of a Bic pen, called it the soul of him which I'd save for the right idea, and the rest of it I brought to work and on my lunch break brought up to the helipad and in the centre of the H I poured it onto a saucer and placed it down and stood back and waited and watched as gusts of wind sailed puffs of him away, an arm, a leg. A *foot*. And then I took the stupid saucer and I frisbee flung it into the sea.

And now there's still one sailor to come in. Destremeau. I seriously wonder if James didn't die on purpose when he did so that just in case there was some afterlife where the afterliving can influence this world, he figured he'd throw a massive rogue wave Destremeau's way, not necessarily to kill, but almost, almost perhaps enough. Or maybe he'd haunt his ship, freak the shit out of him, drive him mad and make him jump off the stern of his boat and drown without a sound or a word, leaving everyone to wonder what the fuck. Give the story some real drama and tension. Some tragedy. Poetry.

I like to think that that's what he's done for me, but that's way too sentimental, and his dying just makes me sad. But, I guess, also somehow hopeful. Over the course of this long race none of the sailors involved died, but my James did. And that gets me thinking that he made the ultimate sailorly act for me, to bring the reality of the race alive for me. And that gets me thinking of everyone else who has died over the length of this. And I Google it and learn that in this world of yours and mine, 150 000 people die every day, or about six-thousand an hour. Standing at my bar I look out at my customers and imagine them all pulling a James over the next sixty seconds.

I want to be tragically bereaved, my sailor failing to return. I want to wear away the finish on the floorboards of the upstairs front room of my house that faces the sea. Pacing back and forth, back and forth, like a ferry from shore to shore, singing like Sinead as I wait for my disappeared hero sailor to appear on the horizon and prove me right. Prove me worth it.

Fucking gag. I know.

But still.

What I do do is pull my old bike out of the shed and push it to the bike shop and get them to do a quick tune on it. The tires are too soft and I ask them to put more air in and they say they're at max pressure so I ask for the pump and I do it myself, pumping till they're rock hard. "If you're not living on the edge, you're taking up too much space," I say to the mechanic, and he laughs in a way that makes me feel like I've actually connected with him in some way.

And I go for a long, long ride, bumping and jarring and fast, and I think and I think and I think. And then I don't and I don't and I don't. I pop a couple wheelies, in honour of James and his son.

Now don't tell me, because I don't want to know, what he would say about me being on this plane heading to France. Bic pen in my pocket. Going for Destremeau.

Acknowledgments

A heartfelt thanks to Chris and all at NON for the work they do keeping Canadian literature alive, vivid and vast. And thanks to whatsowhichever part it is of Canadian government that somehow manages to keep funds flowing to NON and other such indie presses. Because isn't it Art that made us and keeps us, human and humane?